Potential
THREAT

BLACK TOWER SECURITY

TARA GRACE
ERICSON

Edited by BH Writing Services & Editing Done Write
Cover Design: Jess Mastorakos
Cover Photo: Deana Coufal Photography, Omaha, Nebraska
Cover Models: Shay and Troy Ransburg

Paperback ISBN-13: 978-1-949896-37-4
Ebook ISBN-13: 978-1-949896-38-1

To my readers.
When I want to give up, you remind me of my why.

And to Gabbi, for so many reasons.

"Give thanks to the Lord, for he is Good, for his steadfast love endures forever."

Psalms 136:1

CONTENTS

CHAPTER
ONE

RYDER TUGGED at the neck of his dress shirt for the hundredth time. What was it about weddings that demanded tuxedos? Even if he did feel a bit like James Bond, he wouldn't be signing up to wear one every day.

But he would do anything for his best friend, Flint Raven–even wear a monkey suit.

His glance slid over to where Flint and Jessica were cutting the cake. It had been a beautiful ceremony, not that he had much to compare it to. Ross's small wedding at a dinky farm in Indiana had been a few months ago. It was very different from this glitzy reception. No doubt due to Flint's past life as a billionaire tech CEO, the room was filled with powerful people.

Fame and fortune.

Which was fitting, because he had spent most of the ceremony and the reception trying not to stare at Flint's little sister.

Fiona Raven was the definition of off-limits. Famous and successful in her own right. Once again, his eyes searched until he found her, attentively standing in the circle of guests around the cake-cutting. Exactly where she was expected to be. He knew from experience that Fiona always did what was expected.

And dang, if that didn't make him want to see if he could get her to step out of line. Just once.

Fiona looked stunning in the floor-length dress, the dark-green color making her eyes sparkle. And her bare shoulders? They'd been making him wonder what her skin would feel like all day. When she'd tucked her hand around his elbow to walk down the aisle during the rehearsal, the most incredible blush had risen to her cheeks.

She glanced up, her eyes meeting his across the crowd. He winked at her, and the blush on her cheeks made a delightful reappearance, like it had several times today.

He looked away from her as the DJ announced the first dance. Everyone cheered as Flint escorted Jessica onto the dance floor. The lights turned down, and romantic music swelled.

He probably shouldn't be trying to rattle Fiona. He knew it couldn't go anywhere. Ryder was thrilled for his friend, but he also couldn't shake the feeling that he didn't belong here. For the last seven years, Ryder had been jumping from private security gig to private security gig. Being a paid security consultant for a Colombian drug lord didn't exactly make for good small-talk.

After leaving the NYPD, it had been easier to put his SWAT skills to use doing whatever paid the most. And unfortunately, he'd learned pretty quickly that it was usually the wrong side of the law.

He had agreed to work for Black Tower Security, the firm Flint and Ross were starting up, but they were still a few months away from needing him. If it were up to him, he'd never step foot in Colombia again. Probably better for his long-term survival anyway.

Frustrated with his own broodiness, Ryder grabbed his drink and made a beeline for the exit. He touched Fiona's arm on his way past her and signaled her to follow. She smiled and trailed after him. Was she too polite to say no? No, perhaps it was more than that. They'd been skirting the edge of outright flirtation all day.

When they were both outside the event center, Fiona laughed at his antics as he spun around, singing along–poorly–with the first dance song that they could still hear. "Stop making me laugh, Ryder!" She giggled as he belted the lyrics louder still. "What are we doing out here?"

He shrugged and offered her a drink, which she declined with a simple shake of her head. "Just needed some air. Didn't you need some air? There's like a thousand people in there."

Fiona rolled her eyes. "There are 312 guests."

Of course, she knew. She was the maid of honor. She would know every detail of this wedding. Probably better than Flint did, and it was his wedding.

"Whatever. It's too many."

Fiona wrapped her arms around herself, but he grabbed her hand and pulled her into himself. As they swayed to the romantic song, he soaked in the feel of holding her close. Her head rested on his shoulder.

"It's a nice wedding." Her words hummed against his chest.

He glanced back toward the doors. "Yeah. It is. I'm happy for them." He loved Flint like a brother. Sometimes more than he loved his brother, probably.

The fact that he and Jessica had finally found their second chance was exactly what Flint had needed.

"Me too. They deserve it." She glanced up at him. "I heard you were part of the team that rescued Jessica that day."

He shrugged. "No big deal." He remembered the frantic calls from Flint. His role was a small one, but one he'd been eager to play. If something had happened to Jessica, it would have destroyed his best friend. When she'd uncovered a money laundering scheme and ultimately been kidnapped, Flint had dropped everything to save her. And Ryder had dropped everything to help him.

"It is a big deal," she argued. "You and my brother… You've always been so close." Her tone was wistful.

"Since college," he confirmed. An awkward silence fell over them for a few moments.

She pulled away slightly. "I should head back inside," she said, turning toward the door.

He wasn't ready to see her go. "Do you always do what you're supposed to?"

She paused and looked back at him, chin tipped up. "Usually. Why? Don't you?"

Ryder flashed a mischievous grin. "Hardly." His eyes slipped past her to the car sitting directly in front of the event center. It was a thing of beauty. A 1965 Ford Shelby Mustang… Flint had bought it a few years back and he loved that car. Almost as much as he loved Jessica.

"Take the car with me," he blurted. His grin widened. This was exactly what he needed. The adrenaline was already starting to course through his system. He could see it now. He and Fiona, whipping down the freeway in the slick little sports car.

"Are you out of your mind?" Fiona's tone of absolute incredulity brought his daydream to an abrupt halt. She laughed nervously.

He stepped closer and grabbed her hand again. "Come on. You know you want to."

She shook her head, but he saw the hesitation in her eyes. She should say no. He shouldn't press. But he didn't like *shoulds*.

"Come with me," he said.

She looked at the car and then back at him. He saw the moment her mind was made up, and watched the light dim and the hint of excitement and laughter die. She shook her head and pulled her hand from his. "I can't do that. And you shouldn't either."

Frustration rose and he lashed out. "Be spontaneous for once in your life, Fiona."

She tipped her chin and turned toward the door. "Spontaneity is simply irresponsibility in disguise."

Her words stung. Ryder watched as she slipped inside, cool and collected and not a hair out of place. Not like he'd hoped to see her. Laughing and carefree and tendrils of hair escaping from the intricate style.

Irresponsible? She had wanted to come. And if she wasn't willing to have a good time, he'd do it himself.

He snuck back into the small meeting room the groomsmen had used to get ready for the wedding and rifled through Flint's things until he found the keys. The ride would have been better with Fiona in the passenger seat, but he wasn't going to let her ruin his fun.

———

Fiona pressed her lips together, watching Flint lecture Ryder. It wouldn't do to laugh, so she didn't.

He looked like a little kid who got called to the principal's office. Truthfully, he looked fairly chagrined. Despite his shameful countenance, his eyes flashed to hers, and he winked before turning his attention back to Flint and schooling his features.

She hid her laughter by scratching her cheek.

Fiona had been an inch away from agreeing to go with Ryder last night. The mysterious best friend of her older brother, Ryder was the quintessential bad boy. Dangerous, to be sure.

He made her want to forget her responsibilities and let loose. When he'd held her tight and danced in the moonlight, her resolve had nearly melted.

But even as much as she'd wanted to say yes, she'd been acutely aware of what people would say and think. And just like that, her decision had been made.

Consequences like last night's uproar and this morning's argument were exactly why she couldn't do that. The police had tried to be discreet, but uniformed officers couldn't exactly blend in at a black-tie event.

"When will you grow up, Mac?" Her brother's tone betrayed his usual unflappable patience.

"It was just a joke. I didn't expect to get pulled over. Let alone that they would assume I had stolen the car and call you."

"They didn't just call. They came to the wedding! Do you have any idea how embarrassing it was for the police to show up at the reception?"

Their conversation took place in the next room, and Fiona busied herself adjusting the food being served for brunch. The wedding party and close family would be here for one last wedding festivity.

As she eavesdropped, the men worked it out and hugged, complete with claps on the back like guy friends did.

Ryder sauntered into the kitchen and snagged a strawberry from the fruit tray.

"Sounds like you had a fun night," she said with a cheeky smile.

"It would have been more fun if you were there," he said before biting into the red berry.

Heat crept up Fiona's neck, and she shook her head. She had to remind herself that she made the right decision. Fiona Raven could not make a scene at her brother's wedding, and the fact that she'd almost considered it was proof that Ryder McClain was very dangerous.

On Monday, she would return to New York and the headquarters of Raven Foods. And Ryder would go back to whatever it was he did. She was better off forgetting about their flirtatious banter yesterday.

Even if she wasn't sure she could ever forget that dance.

CHAPTER
TWO

3 YEARS LATER

RYDER MCCLAIN CHUCKED his duffle bag into the corner of the locker room at Black Tower Security and collapsed on the padded bench. He'd been biting back his frustration for the entire hour-long van ride home, but it got the best of him now.

Everything had worked out fine. It was a good thing he worked with some of the best in the business. Otherwise, today could have gone much, much worse.

"Ryder," Flint got his attention. "Hit the shower and then come see me."

His friend's tone wasn't harsh, but it wasn't exactly kind either. Ryder looked up from the spot on the floor he was staring at and met Flint's gaze across the room. He jerked his head up in acknowledgement. Order received.

Around him, his team members hung their gear in the spacious lockers and unlaced their boots. Jackson Kelly and his brother, Marshall, were deep in a debate about whether *Die Hard* counted as a Christmas movie.

His buddy, Tank, made his way over. The arms on the massive man stretched the fabric of his black T-shirt. Tank was like Dwayne Johnson and Vin Diesel combined. Except with hair. "You okay, Mac?" Oh, and a heart of gold hiding behind all the muscle and intimidating demeanor.

He put on a tight smile. "Why wouldn't I be? Thanks for the save out there, man."

Tank looked surprised. "Of course. We got each other's back, right?"

"Always," Ryder confirmed. It was the truth. He would gladly lay down his life for any one of the people he worked with at Black Tower Security. He may have joined for his own reasons, but over the last three years, BTS had become family.

The NYPD had been a brotherhood too, but it was different from the tight-knit group at BTS. At the

NYPD, the loyalty was to the badge. You might not even know the person behind it. After he'd lost his job, it seemed like he might as well have never existed to his brothers there.

Black Tower had been around for just a few years, but he knew these men and women as well as he knew himself. And that loyalty would carry outside these walls whenever needed.

Tank shrugged. "Besides, if you hadn't called out that sniper, they would have wiped us out one by one. This whole mission could have gone up in flames without you, Mac."

Jackson sauntered over, a towel hung around his bare shoulders. "Tank's right, man. You really saved our tails out there."

Ryder nodded weakly. "Thanks, guys. I still wish it had gone differently." Despite his best efforts, Flint had been shot, and the sniper had gotten away. The flash of light off the scope had tipped him off with only seconds to spare.

So why was he upset? The kicker was he'd felt the eyes of the sniper earlier and ignored it.

Jackson clapped a heavy hand on Ryder's shoulder. "We all do our best in the moment. It doesn't do any good to second-guess decisions made in the heat of battle."

"Yeah. I know." That wouldn't stop Ryder from reliving every mission, wondering if he'd done the right thing. At least now that he was with BTS, he knew he was fighting for the right side.

He nudged the temperature on the shower dial hotter, until it began to ease the sore muscles in his back and shoulders. While he appreciated Tank tackling him out of the way of that bullet, being driven into the ground by the former linebacker would leave him with bruises the size of footballs.

He dried off and got dressed. Since the very process of pulling on a shirt made him want to groan, he shook a generous dose of painkillers into his hand, downing them with a chaser of Powerade. When he knocked on Flint's door, he found Jessica checking the bandage on Flint's arm.

When Tank had pushed Ryder out of the way, Flint had caught a ricochet bullet off the armored vehicle.

"How's it look?"

"Not bad at all. Just a graze," she answered.

"My nurse thinks I'll live," Flint joked.

Ryder was always amazed by the way she supported Flint. Not every wife would be okay with her husband putting himself in the line of fire. It probably had something to do with how he and the team had rescued her from a kidnapping before Black Tower Security even existed.

It had been her kidnapping and rescue that had driven the three of them to start BTS. One of the goals of the organization was to help those who didn't have the resources to help themselves. Ryder's brother, Ross, was former Secret Service and the co-owner of Black Tower. Actually, Flint and Ross were co-owners. Ryder had just come along for the ride as the first employee. Waiting for them to need him while he was still finishing his last contract had been the longest year of his life.

Flint kissed Jessica's hand. "Can you give us a minute?"

After Jessica left, he came around the desk and sat on the edge. "You okay?"

Ryder shook his head. "I'm good."

When there was no response, he turned to find the familiar patient look on his friend's face.

A knock on the door sounded before Ross stuck his head in. "Hey."

Ryder sat back and rolled his eyes behind closed lids. Here came his perfect brother to dole out words of wisdom. Yay. "Double-teaming me?"

"We just want to talk about what happened," Flint said.

Ryder sat up and jerked a shoulder. "I screwed up, okay? I don't know what else to say. I knew there was something off, but I couldn't figure out what it was. By the time I realized there was a sniper, it was almost too late."

Flint laid a hand on his shoulder. "Everybody on this team knows they can count on you. Except you. You can trust your instincts, Mac. The rest of us do. Without your heads up, we might have had multiple casualties–including you.

Ross chimed in. "You should be celebrating! In the end, you made the right call this time. You're letting your past mess with your head."

Ryder scoffed. "Oh, and what would you know about it? You've always made the right choice, saved the day, got the girl, and ridden off into the sunset."

His brother raised an eyebrow. "Andi would kick your tail if she heard you talk about her like a carnival prize."

A smile tugged at Ryder's cheek. His brother was right. Ross had married Andi three years ago when they started BTS, and she was every bit as tough as anyone Ryder had ever met. "True. I'm just saying… It always seems to work out for you. Perimeter security was my responsibility, and I was almost too late."

Ross shook his head sadly. "I think you're forgetting a few things. It hasn't always worked out for me."

A wave of shame washed over him. Before Andi, Ross had been engaged to another woman. While he was away on an assignment, Candace had been killed by a stalker. "You're right. I'm sorry. It's easy to focus on the things I'm envious of. I'm just frustrated that I didn't catch it sooner."

Ross frowned. "Sure, you've made your share of mistakes. We all have. But it worked out today. Everybody came home in one piece, and we got the package. But I had a feeling you wouldn't count it as a victory."

"Yeah, well. I don't. Look, I'm tired and I just want to go home and crash." He rolled his shoulder. "Tank is built like…well, a tank."

His two closest friends in the world chuckled.

Flint spoke through his laughter. "Fine. Go home. We're not done with this, though."

Ryder stood and made his way to the door as his sarcastic reply snuck out. "Oh, goodie. More therapy with Dr. Raven. Have you thought about getting your own radio show?"

Flint grabbed a stress ball from his desk and chucked it at Ryder. Instead, it bounced off the wall and smacked Ross in the forehead.

Ryder tipped his head back with a laugh. "Nice reflexes, bro." He ducked into the hallway with a grin on his face.

CHAPTER THREE

FIONA RAVEN FLIPPED OPEN her calendar application and checked her plans for the day. The usual morning meeting with her manufacturing facility outside of Chicago, followed by a call with the editor for her upcoming cookbook, and a lunch at WBC headquarters.

In the afternoon, she had a meeting here at Raven Foods corporate offices to finalize the Winter issue of her magazine, Homestyle Heart. Then a follow-up with the market research team about the opportunity to expand into canned goods. There was a company they were looking to acquire—PrimoPak Foods had all the resources to create a national product line. And none of the branding. The small South Carolina company would be a good addition to her business if it all worked out.

All of that would be topped off with an evening in her personal kitchen, doing her dry-run for the episodes of Rustic Raven she would film in three days.

Of course, that last part wasn't on her calendar. That was her little secret—an extra safeguard to make sure she never made a mistake on set that would tarnish her reputation.

Gabbi, her assistant and best friend, poked her head in with an admonishing look. "Fi, it's only six forty-five. How long have you been here?"

Fiona smiled warmly. "I just got in." It wasn't a lie, but it didn't include the fact that she had spent an hour replying to emails from her computer at home before showering and driving in. Emails that were all scheduled to send at a perfectly respectable hour so no one realized she was working before five a.m. It wouldn't do for anyone to think she couldn't handle everything during normal working hours.

"If you say so." Gabbi stepped in and set a stack of mail on the desk. The colorful blouse she wore was accented with chunky gold jewelry and a bold head-band holding back her naturally curly hair. She handed Fiona a large coffee and looked up from the clipboard in her hand. She stopped in her tracks then blurted out, "Girl, you look tired."

Fiona's mouth dropped, torn between laughter and horror. There was no filter on her fearless friend, something that was both a blessing and a curse at times. Quickly, she grabbed a mirror from her desk drawer. The dark circles under her eyes were especially pronounced. "Oh no! I forgot my concealer!"

Gabbi waved a hand. "You still look great. Don't even worry about it."

Easy for her to say. The New York native had flawless dark-brown skin and an attitude that didn't leave room for anyone to criticize. In a lot of ways, she envied her confidence. Fiona was self-assured, but only because she made one hundred percent sure nothing went wrong.

She pulled her emergency makeup stash from the drawer and fixed the offending shadows, while Gabbi looked on with amusement.

"I'm gonna let you slide on this unreasonable display of vanity." Gabbi raised an eyebrow. "But only because you have that lunch at WBC. Do you know what that's about?"

Fiona's eyes flicked over the small compact mirror to see Gabbi. "A little bird from WBC told me the host for the *Date Night America* Valentine's Day special backed out." And Fiona had immediately dropped not-so-subtle hints about her willingness to fill in. The primetime cooking and lifestyle specials only happened a few times a year, but they were always well-anticipated.

Gabbi's mouth dropped open. "Shut up. No way!"

Fiona grinned. "I know! This could be huge."

"Beyond huge," Gabbi agreed. "I'll make sure you've got plenty of time to get there. Want me to reschedule the video call with James?"

Pushing the meeting with the cookbook editor would help, but she also didn't have a slot to put him back in. "See if he can chat at 9:30 instead of 10. I can have Chicago give me the short version." Their meeting about production at the Chicago manufacturing facility happened each morning to review the previous day. She didn't like to miss it, but there wasn't usually anything earth-shattering. This call with WBC could be the key to taking her to the next level.

"On it."

Fiona finished blending the makeup, satisfied with the improved brightness under her eyes. "If he can't change, don't worry about it. I'll make it work."

She always did.

Gabbi left, and Fiona reached eagerly for the caffeine. She guzzled half of it before also picking up the stack of mail.

After taking another drink of coffee, she unfolded and read the top letter on the stack. The thick, black text on the page made her freeze.

I'll destroy you.

The stainless-steel travel mug slipped from her hand and clattered on the floor, jolting her out of the moment. She rushed to grab the cup and lid, but the contents had already spilled across the floor. Fiona felt her breathing grow rapid and she stared helplessly back toward the paper on her desk, ignoring the spill in front of her.

Gabbi was at her side in an instant, mopping up the mess with paper towels. "Dang, Fi. You need to go back to bed?"

She shook her head and pressed a hand to her pounding chest. "That note. Where did it come from?"

Gabbi frowned. "What note?"

Fiona grabbed the offending paper off the corner of the desk and shoved it into Gabbi's hands.

Gabbi's eyes widened as she read it. "Where'd you get this?"

"What do you mean where'd I get this? I got it from you. It was on that stack of mail you left me!"

Gabbi shook her head. "Uh-uh. No way. I sorted that mail personally no less than fifteen minutes ago. That was not in it."

"Well, then explain how it landed on the top of the stack?"

"I don't know! I stacked your mail. Then I went to get your coffee..." She gasped. "I'm calling security!"

Fiona stilled. "You think someone was up here? Right outside my office?"

Gabbi nodded with a worried look and ran out the door.

Fiona paced while she waited, forcing herself to take slow, deep breaths. It was going to be fine. She just needed to convince herself. They'd see who left the note, escort them out, and it would all go away. Probably some stupid prank. Someone thought they were being funny.

She smoothed the pink fabric of her blazer, then sat back down at her desk. Gabbi returned with a new cup of coffee, and Fiona flashed a grateful smile.

"Thanks, Gab."

"No matter what is going on here, I can't have

you uncaffeinated to schmooze those WBC bigshots!"
She appreciated her friend's recognition that she
needed normalcy in this moment. Gabbi's flair for the
dramatic was nearly the exact opposite of the cool and
collected persona Fiona always strived for. After all,
she'd learned early on not to make a scene.

When Jim Daniels showed up, she greeted him
calmly.

He looked over his glasses at her with a worried
expression. "Gabbi told me what happened, Ms.
Raven. Are you sure you're okay?"

"I'm perfectly fine. It's just some silly note,
right?"

Jim didn't look convinced. He was old enough to
be her father, and she had worked with him long
enough to know he truly cared about her. "I'll pull
security footage and see what I can find. But you need
to be careful."

"They were just trying to scare me. But I don't
scare that easily," she insisted.

Jim took the piece of paper and put it in a Ziploc
bag–an action that had her raising her eyebrows.
"What is this, CSI?"

"Just in case." He moved toward the door. "I'll
post someone at your elevator."

"Entirely unnecessary, Jim." She shook her head.

"How about you do your job and let me do mine?" He wasn't backing down and, only because she could see that fatherly concern in his eyes, she acquiesced.

With a nod of acceptance, she said goodbye to Jim and went back to her desk. As much as she proclaimed her nonchalance to the events of the morning, she couldn't deny that it had shaken her up.

Fiona lost herself in the digital pages of the draft cookbook she was supposed to discuss with James later this morning. Her cell phone rang, pulling her away from the computer to grab it. Her brother's name flashed on the screen. She checked the time, then answered.

"It's not a great time, Flint. I've got about five minutes." She took a drink of coffee and made a face at the lukewarm temperature.

"Good morning to you, too."

She winced at his admonishment. "Sorry. You're right, that was rude. Let me try again. How are you? How's Jessica?"

"We are both good. Looking forward to seeing you next week."

She wracked her brain and then spoke. "Right, next week. Christmas."

Flint clicked his tongue. "Don't tell me you forgot about Christmas."

"I didn't forget. I just hadn't looked at my calendar yet." She didn't mention that she was pretty sure it wasn't written on the calendar.

"Well, Jessie has the guest room all made up. I just wanted to make sure you were still coming."

Fiona smiled. "Thanks. I wouldn't miss it."

The trip to Alexandria wouldn't take long, and it would be good for her to get away. Even if it was just a night or two. Any longer than that probably wasn't feasible. Especially if her meeting today went as planned.

She checked her watch. "Sorry, I gotta run. My Chicago plant meeting starts at eight."

"See you next week." The farewell trailed off as she pulled the phone away from her ear and disconnected.

The following week, Fiona curled her legs under her and wrapped her hands around the mug of cocoa, letting the warmth soak into her palms. The lights from the Christmas tree flickered merrily as Jessica teased Flint about the ham he'd fixed.

"I'm just saying, I think eight hours in the crockpot for that little ham was a little bit of overkill."

Jessica looked at her. "You're the chef. Back me up on this."

She loved seeing them like this. Too many people kowtowed to Flint, but Jessica never had. Her brother had never been the same after he and Jessica had parted ways. She and Flint were a lot alike, but she'd never found anyone who made her feel the way he did about Jessica.

Fiona shook her head. "I never complain when someone cooks for me. It's a personal rule."

"So it was good?" Flint looked at her with a mischievous smile.

She narrowed her eyes at him. He was trying to trap her into lying or saying something rude. She would do neither. "It was so kind of you to host Christmas dinner."

He chuckled, a warm, low sound that carried across the cozy living room. "So diplomatic. I know I killed the poor ham. I just wondered who loved me enough to tell me the truth."

"You know I'll always tell you when you mess up," Jessica said with a laugh. He brought her a drink, and she tipped her head up for a kiss.

After kissing his wife, Flint flopped down on the other side of the couch. "How's work, Fi?"

Fiona shifted. "It's really crazy, but going so well. WBC asked me to host *Date Night America* for Valentine's Day." She'd been basking in the high that came with the invitation for a week now. And going a bit crazy making room for all the preparation in her schedule.

"Wow, that's awesome. You're going to do great. When did you find out?" Flint's voice was proud and Fiona soaked in the praise. She was proud, too.

"Just last week. Actually, the same day you called me. Other than a weird note I got that morning, it was kind of a banner day. I approved my next cookbook and got the offer for the WBC special on the same day."

"What weird note?"

Oops. She could hear the protective curiosity in Flint's voice. "Uh-uh. Don't do that."

He looked confused. "Do what?"

She frowned at him. "Get all big brother on me. It was just a weird note. My security team is taking care of it."

"What did it say?"

Fiona paused, torn between her desire to be honest and her desire to keep Flint out of her business. "It said they would destroy me," she finally admitted.

"What the heck? You didn't tell me?"

His intense reaction made her squirm. He seemed

really worried. She told him the same thing she'd been saying to herself since it happened. "It's no big deal, Flint. Security has it covered."

"They found the guy?"

"Well, no. Not exactly. The camera footage of my floor was corrupted or something." She waved her hand. "It's fine."

"It doesn't sound like it. That doesn't sound like something to just brush off." Flint gave her his trade-mark serious look. "Has anything else happened?"

Fiona resisted the urge to wither under his assess-ment. "Someone tried to get into my condo. But the security team flagged it and didn't let him in."

"He got away?"

She nodded. "Yeah. They said he took off when they started asking questions."

Flint shook his head and crossed his arms. "You should have told me."

"I'm fine! I don't need my big brother to protect me."

"You apparently need someone!" Ah, there was that intimidating Italian temper. "I get it, sis. You are independent, and I'm so proud of your success. But I don't care about all of that. I care about you. I'm assigning one of my guys."

She sat up abruptly. "Absolutely not! I don't need

a babysitter, *fratellone*." The Italian slipped in, a relic of their Italian-native parents.

"Mac is a bodyguard, Fi. Not a babysitter."

She stilled. "Ryder?" She hadn't seen him since the wedding. When he'd almost made her lose her better judgment. She shook her head firmly. "You can't send Ryder to be my bodyguard!"

Flint leaned back against the leather and kicked a leg over his knee. "Sure, I can. I'm his boss."

Fiona rolled her eyes at her brother's matter-of-fact statement. "I don't need a bodyguard. Besides, isn't Black Tower supposed to be helping those who can't help themselves?"

"I guess I'll have to modify that part of the mission statement to be can't *or won't.*" His irritation was displayed prominently in the pointed look he gave her.

She opened her mouth to argue again, but Flint cut her off. "Please, Fi. I know you say you don't need it, but if I don't send someone, I'll just worry about you. Do it for me?" He shamelessly turned his puppy-dog expression on her.

She took a deep breath. "Fine." At his expression of victory, she held up a hand. "But—he stays out of my offices. He can guard me in public. But I've got my own security team at work and I don't need him following me around there."

"I'll take it," Flint said.

Fiona sipped her hot cocoa with a sigh. She wasn't sure what would be more dangerous: the mysterious threat or Ryder McClain as an everyday figure in her life.

CHAPTER FOUR

RYDER PRESSED THE WEIGHTS UP, focusing on his breath as he finished the last set. The weight caused his arms to shake as he struggled with the tenth repetition. The gym at BTS headquarters was state of the art, and Jessica was their personal trainer. And she didn't take it easy on them. She always increased their weight sets just enough to make the workout a challenge. Something he didn't usually appreciate in the moment.

The face that appeared above him wasn't Jessica's though.

"You got a minute?" Flint's dark features floated above him.

Ryder groaned as he pushed the bar on the rack and panted an acknowledgement. He sat up, wiping his hands on a towel, and then his forehead, trying to stay neutral. If this was more lecturing about the last mission, he was going to lose his mind.

The truth was that whatever Flint had to say, Ryder knew he would listen. Flint was the closest friend he'd ever had, and he'd gotten Ryder out of more than a few scrapes over the years.

There was nothing Ryder wouldn't do for Flint. But judging by the look on his friend's face, he might come to regret that particular feeling.

Ryder drank his water and waited.

Flint sat across from him on the next workout bench over. "You still have your New York City Pistol License?"

Ryder nodded slowly. "Yeah." Leaving the NYPD and working some private security jobs in the city meant he still had permission to carry a gun in one of the most restrictive cities in the country. "It'd be more hassle than it's worth to let it lapse and have to get a new one someday. Why?"

"It's about Fiona."

Ryder swallowed and wiped his mouth with the back of his arm. "Is she okay?" Fiona was… Well, Fiona was Flint's little sister. And Flint was like his brother. That was as far as it could go.

"She's okay for now. But there's been a few threats, so I'm sending her some extra protection."

Threats didn't sound good. But Fiona was a big girl. Not to mention she was nearly as financially successful as her brother. This sounded like Flint playing protective big brother.

Ryder smirked. "I bet she loves that."

Flint rubbed the back of his neck and winced. "Not exactly. Which is why I'm sending you."

"Rave, no." He tipped his head back.

"It's not optional, Mac. I need someone I can count on there. She's my sister, and she's stubborn enough to make things difficult."

"Hmm, I wonder where she gets that…" He gave Flint a pointed glance.

"Who, me?" When their laughter faded, Flint's smile disappeared, his expression solemn. "I need your help."

"You should choose someone else. I'm not the guy for this." The ghosts of the previous mission were fresh in his mind.

Flint shook his head adamantly. "Yes, you are. There is no one I would trust to take care of Fiona more than I trust you. You're my brother, Mac. And I know you'll do whatever it takes to protect her."

Ryder stared at the towel in his hands. The confidence Flint had in him was misplaced. But he wasn't wrong that Ryder would do everything he could to protect Fiona. He just wasn't sure it would be enough. He had a history of making the wrong decision at the wrong time. Decisions that had changed the course of his entire life and led him down paths he never should have walked.

"I'm asking you to find someone else."

"And I'm telling you there is no one else. You're my guy. I would go myself, but with Jessie pregnant, I can't exactly leave her here."

"What? Jessica's pregnant?"

Flint's smile was enormous when he replied. "She's still early on, but she's been really sick."

Across the room, his friend's wife sat on one of the weight lifting benches. She definitely hadn't been her usual demanding self during their last few workouts. Apparently, now he knew why. Good for them.

"Congratulations, man." He stood and hugged his best friend, clapping him on the back. Flint and Jessica had something special. "Wow. You're going to be a dad. That's wild."

"Thanks. I guess you'll be Uncle Mac." Flint's hand rested heavy on Ryder's shoulder as they stood talking. "But you see why you have to go? I don't trust anyone else the way I trust you." He wasn't backing down.

Despite the sinking feeling in his chest, Ryder bobbed his head. "Okay."

If Fiona was in trouble, he would get to the bottom of it. And he would make sure he kept her safe. He wasn't going to let his friend down.

Flint pointed at him as he started walking away. "I owe you, man."

"I'll add it to your tally," he ribbed.

"Just remember, keep Fi close, but not too close, got it? Don't be getting any ideas about my little sister."

Flint's smile was casual, but Ryder nodded. "Of course not. She's like my sister, too!" He tried to convey the ridiculousness of the warning with his voice. In response, Flint waved as he turned around completely and headed toward Jessica.

The warning was a good reminder. As much as Flint trusted Ryder to take care of Fiona, he still wasn't good enough to be with her romantically. Not that Ryder disagreed.

Fiona was perfect.

Proper.

Good.

And he…was not. Perfect, proper, or good.

He'd been paid by the wrong side a few too many times to feel like he could be a hero anymore.

It would serve him well to remember that. If his stunt at Flint's wedding was any indicator, being around Fiona made him forget his place. His crazy idea had only been dreamed up because of the reaction it would get from her. When she'd said no? His own stubborn side wouldn't let him ditch the plan. He'd gotten caught up in the way he could make her eyes dance with laughter.

And dance they had when Flint had lectured him the following morning at brunch. Even better? The way the blush had risen in her cheeks when he'd winked at her during Flint's tirade. Fiona Raven made him want to simultaneously be a man good enough for her and corrupt her just enough to prove she wasn't perfect after all.

She was a dangerous combination. But if she was in danger? He'd keep his head in the game. He had to.

CHAPTER FIVE

FIONA SPOONED the pasta into a large white serving bowl, then sprinkled a handful of fresh parsley on it before smiling into the camera. The deep-red Bolognese sauce contrasted with the white bowl, which had been carefully selected for the most appealing presentation.

"That's all there is to it. Serve this along with some crusty bread and high-quality olive oil and your guests are sure to enjoy. That's all the time we have today on Rustic Raven. Join me next time when I'll be making a bourguignon-inspired Italian beef stew that is guaranteed to warm up any chilly winter day. *Alla Prossima*. Until next time, my friends. Eat well and be happy."

She smiled warmly, until the director's voice rang

through the studio. "Cut! Okay, let's take another shot of filling and garnishing the bowl, and then we're set."

She nodded and then faltered as she noticed a familiar face among the crew. In the dim lights off set, she could make out his features. Chiseled chin, piercing eyes.

Ryder McClain.

He leaned against a pillar like a book slightly askew on a library shelf. Not like one who was out of place, just comfortably biding its time. Ryder seemed accustomed to making himself comfortable, no matter the circumstances.

Her hands shook as she poured the pasta back into the pan and set it on the stove. An assistant placed a clean, identical serving dish on the counter.

Why did it make her nervous that he was here? She had known he was coming. It was good she hadn't seen him during the farewell script, or the entire take would have been trashed. Her heart was racing, like it had the very first time she'd filmed an episode.

She took a deep breath. She was being ridiculous.

Fiona waited for the cameras to come close. On her cue, she lifted the pot and poured the contents into the bright porcelain bowl, careful to position her hands so the camera would have the best shot. Then, she reached and re-reached for the chopped parsley and sprinkled it over the bowl, taking ample time.

"Got it?"

The cameraman nodded. "Got it."

The director clapped. "That's it. Clean the set and we'll start again in twenty minutes."

A handful of assistants took over, quickly clearing the counters, dishes, and removing the prop decor. The fresh flowers or fruit were carefully selected and cycled to make it seem like this was truly Fiona's home kitchen–and that five episodes weren't shot back-to-back.

She walked off the set, willing her heart to slow. "Hello, Ryder."

He wore a tan leather jacket, at least three days of scruff, and a crooked smile. Yep, he was dangerous. "Fiona Raven. Long time no see."

The way he said her name made her toes curl. His midwestern Iowa drawl was so different from the clipped New York accent so common around here.

She took a deep breath. "Just so you know, I tried to talk my brother out of this." She flashed him a smile.

"Just so you know, so did I. But he sounded pretty worried."

She waved a hand. "It's not a big deal. Honestly, it's probably a waste of your time."

Ryder shrugged. "Flint doesn't think so. And he told me to come, so here I am."

"Do you always do what people tell you?" That didn't sound like the Ryder she knew. If that were the case, he'd have never stolen that car at the wedding.

He raised an eyebrow. "People? No." He shrugged. "Flint? If I can. He's never steered me wrong. Usually, I handle that part myself."

Fiona didn't know how to reply to that cryptic comment. She ran her hands down her shirt. "Oh, I actually better go change. We've got one last episode to tape. Then I'll show you around, okay?"

"Works for me." He stuck his hands in the pockets of his jacket and resumed leaning against the pillar.

She looked around for a way to make him more comfortable. So he wouldn't be watching her the entire time. She'd never be able to concentrate knowing he was there. "You can, umm, wait wherever. There is a green room in the back. You don't have to watch."

"I don't mind. I've seen the show. It'll be interesting to see how the sausage is made."

Fiona frowned. "We're not making sausage today. I did that last season."

He chuckled. "I just mean it'll be cool to see behind the scenes."

"Oh." Of course, it was a figure of speech. She knew that. Why wasn't her brain working?

With that awkward exchange haunting her, she went backstage and quickly changed clothes. The makeup artist added a clip to her hair and refreshed the powder on her nose and forehead.

She grabbed the notecard for the episode they were taping next and reviewed the recipes. She already knew them by heart, and she'd done a dry run of each episode on her own several weeks ago.

But those were dress rehearsals. This was the performance. And even though it was extensively edited, Fiona wanted it to be perfect.

The director had often commented how easy her show was to produce compared to others. She rarely stumbled on her words and never made a mistake that would warrant an extensive retake.

She made sure of it.

When she stepped back onto set, the bouquet of autumn-colored blooms had been replaced with a bowl of gourds and pinecones. They'd already filmed the episodes that would air next spring and summer and were now working on the shows for fall.

She stepped to her mark and smiled broadly into

the camera. Time to be the Fiona Raven everyone knew and loved.

————

Ryder watched with curiosity as Fiona confidently turned raw vegetables, meat, and wine into something that made the whole set smell even more delicious than the pasta dish that had his stomach growling an hour ago.

She made it look effortless, cooking even while she talked to the cameras as though they were her best friends. He could see why her show had such good ratings. Women who watched it felt like they were over at her house for coffee and lunch. Heck, *he* felt like he was at her house for lunch, other than the fifteen other people standing around.

Every few minutes, the director interrupted and had her reshoot actions or repeat lines, but Fiona never showed frustration or fatigue. He could see it when he watched closely though. It was hiding in the way her shoulders pulled slightly to the front when the cameras weren't rolling, but they always straightened again.

When she finished with her signature goodbye,

her accent unchecked on the Italian phrase, Ryder stood up from where he leaned against the wall.

The director spoke loudly to the crew, "That's a wrap. Clear the set. We'll go again next week for the Thanksgiving and Christmas episodes."

Fiona called above the noise, "Thanks, everyone. As usual, all the food from today's episodes is over at the crafty table!"

The crew applauded her announcement. If it tasted as good as it smelled, he could understand why.

She walked off the set and straight toward him. He really liked being the first one she came to. Probably shouldn't overanalyze that particular feeling. He stepped up to meet her and asked, "What's the crafty table?"

She pointed down the hall. "It's an industry term. It's just the table where we keep coffee and snacks while filming. It takes about ten hours of shooting for us to get five episodes filmed."

Fiona walked him through a quick tour of the studio, which took up the entire third floor of the building between wardrobe, makeup, and prop storage. He followed her through endless hallways, her high heels clicking on the tile floors in a steady rhythm as she explained everything about how her show was filmed and produced in-house so Raven Foods retained all the rights to it.

"Which came first, the show or the food?"

She smiled. "Common misconception. Actually, first came the blog. I started it when I was in culinary school." Laughter filled her voice when she explained, "I remember staying up all night testing six different blueberry muffin recipes so I would pick the very best one for the following day's blog post."

She hit the button on the elevator. "The blog did well, and I was approached by an agent. She brought the cooking show. I started the magazine as a way to reach viewers who wanted something offline. Then, the pre-packaged foods business was an acquisition and a revamp of an existing facility."

As they took the elevator to the rest of the corporate office, Ryder reevaluated what he knew about Fiona Raven. It wasn't just that she was kind and always seemed to say or do the right thing. She also worked really stinking hard to achieve her dreams.

"I don't know why I'm showing you all of this. I made it very clear to Flint that I won't have you lurking around the office, scaring the staff."

Ryder tried to hide his smile. "I don't lurk."

"Oh, you definitely lurk."

He wanted to press her further, make her blush

with a flirty comment. Instead, he simply shrugged. "We'll see how it goes. If I have to be in your office to protect you, then I'm going to be in your office."

Fiona looked like she wanted to object. But she just gave him a tight smile. "Fine. Let's go talk to Daniels. He is in charge of security for the building."

Ryder followed wordlessly. People waved and smiled at Fiona as they made their way through the building. He was amazed at how many people she knew by name, even asking them about their family or some project for the company.

The security team was no different.

"Ms. Raven, good to see you!"

"Hey Jim. Jim, this is Ryder McClain. He's private security that I've hired due to the threats. Ryder, this is Jim Daniels, my head of corporate security."

Oh, now *she* had hired him? Ryder watched the man's face, but saw nothing but a hint of surprise at the revelation that Ryder would be working private security. "Nice to meet you, Jim."

"Same goes, Mr. McClain."

"Call me Mac." It was an easy way to establish rapport with the man. Besides, being called Mr. McClain made him cringe. It was just a step away from Agent McClain…and he was as far away from his goody-two-shoes big brother as he could get.

"All right, Mac. I'm glad you're taking care of Ms. Raven. I tried to get her to assign one of my guys to a personal detail, but she wouldn't hear of it. Corporate resources, yadda yadda."

He raised an eyebrow at Fiona. She shrugged. "The company's security is to protect the company. Not me."

"From what I can see, you *are* the company."

Fiona waved a hand. "I'm the face, sure. But my goal is that Raven Foods will live on long after I'm gone."

Daniels reached for a file on his desk. "Whoever it is, I'm glad you've got someone watching your back. I don't have a good feeling about this."

Ryder took the folder extended to him and flipped it open. The note he'd heard about but not seen. It was jarring to see the threat in black and white. Big, block letters contrasted starkly against the crisp white paper. There was a CD labeled with "15th floor, December 12th" and computer access logs from the same morning.

He looked up at Daniels. "Any lead on the security cameras?"

Jim shook his head. "Unfortunately, no. Best we

can tell, they got a backdoor into the system and killed the connection to those cameras for about two hours that morning."

He turned to Fiona. "What about the breach at your condo?"

"We'll have to get it from them. I hadn't actually brought that to the team here."

Ryder bit back his frustration. By attacking on two fronts, the culprit had successfully prevented the information from being connected by any one person. "I'll go there next." He held up the folder. "Thanks for this, Jim. I'll keep you posted?"

"Sounds good. We're here to do whatever you need. I agree with you–Ms. Raven IS Raven Foods and we have to protect her."

"And Ms. Raven can hear you talking about her," Fiona chided. "Ryder—I mean, Mac will be responsible for my security when I am not in the building. You will remain my main security while I am here, okay?"

Jim nodded. "On it." Then he met Ryder's eyes. "I guess I'll keep you posted as well."

Ryder grunted in response and made his exit from the small security command center. Daniels seemed like a good guy. He pulled out his phone and sent a text to Joey.

RM: I need a background on Jim Daniels. Works security at Raven Foods.

JR: On it.

His gut told him he could trust Daniels. But he wasn't going to take any chances that his gut was wrong. Asking their tech and intel specialist, Joey Rodriguez, would make sure of it. Joey—or Josephina, if someone felt like making an enemy of the most talented computer hacker he'd ever met— would dig up any skeletons.

CHAPTER
SIX

FIONA STOOD ANXIOUSLY inside the elevator with Ryder, on the long ride up to her penthouse condominium. Neither of them spoke, but she felt like the air was as thick as the balsamic she drizzled on rich, creamy pastas.

Like the last two nights, they walked to her door and she unlocked it. Ryder pulled a pistol from the holster under his jacket and went inside while she stood impatiently in the hallway. He insisted on checking out the condo before he'd let her go inside.

Tonight, Gabbi was picking up dinner on her way to hang out for the evening. Fiona's stomach growled at the thought of the Vietnamese food from the place down the block.

Ryder stepped back out. "All clear."

"Obviously," she said snarkily before pushing past him.

"I'll see you in the morning. Six o'clock?"

"Yep," she responded coolly as she placed her bags carefully on the hooks by the door and busied herself removing her shoes. She was annoyed. He was just doing his job. But his job was interfering with her life, and it was aggravating.

"Fi?" When she looked, Ryder stood in the doorway. "I'm right down the street if you need anything."

"I won't."

He nodded. "I hope not." Then he shut the door and she was blissfully alone for the first time all day. Desperate for air, she stepped out on the balcony and took a deep breath, allowing the busyness of the day to drift away, swallowed by the ambient noise of the traffic below.

A sound behind her made her turn, and she saw Gabbi walking through the door with bags of food. But something else caught her eye as well. The dark square blocked her view into the rest of the condo and she went over to it.

It was a paper, taped to the outside of her balcony window.

They can't protect you.

Fiona shrieked and ran inside, shutting and locking the balcony door behind her.

"Where's the fire, Fi?" Gabbi's laughing tone disappeared after she saw Fiona's face. "Oh my word, what happened?"

Fiona sat on the couch and pointed at the balcony. Gabbi went to investigate.

"You've gotta call Mac."

Fiona shook her head. "No. He was just here. The apartment is clear. He just missed the note." And after the cold way she'd been treating him, the last thing she wanted to do was eat crow and reveal that she really did need him. "I'll tell him tomorrow."

Gabbi frowned at her. "Why don't I believe that?"

"I will!" Fiona reassured her. "It's fine. It's just a note. And it wasn't even inside the apartment." She was grasping at straws here, but it didn't matter.

"Yeah, a note on the balcony of your condo on *the 90th floor*. You think Spiderman is your stalker or what?"

Fiona shook her head. "I don't know. I just need some time to process this before Ryder gets all involved."

Gabbi watched her silently. "Fine, but I'm staying the night."

Fiona gave her a grateful smile. "Thanks, Gab. You're the best."

"And you're being a dummy. But I still love you."

Fiona laughed, despite the adrenaline that still had her a bit shaky. She wasn't sure how she had been lucky enough to get Gabbi on her side, but she would never stop thanking God that she had.

———

Ryder sat at the same table he'd sat in all day yesterday. And the day before that. Since Fiona wouldn't let him provide security while she was at the office, he had claimed a spot at the small coffee shop on the main floor of the corporate office. The coffee shop was open to the public but mostly catered to the employees who worked in the offices above.

Most importantly for him, it provided an unob-structed view of the Raven Foods lobby and meant he was able to drop Fiona off and pick her back up.

Maybe he should tell Fiona her coffee shop needed more comfortable chairs.

He spotted Fiona's friend, Gabbi, striding across the lobby and checked his watch. She usually came down about thirty minutes after Fiona got to the office, and then again around lunch. But it was only ten fifteen.

She headed straight for him and he sat up. "Is everything okay? Where's Fiona?"

Gabbi sat down, glancing around like she was nervous someone would see her. His pulse started to race.

"Fi would kill me if she knew I was talking to you."

He frowned. "Is she all right?"

"She's fine. Stupid, but fine."

He smirked at her blunt assessment. "Okay?"

"I told her to tell you herself, but she hasn't yet. So here I am."

The way this woman talked around the subject was going to drive him nuts. "Tell me what?"

"There was another note last night. At the apartment."

A surge of adrenaline coursed through his veins. "How?"

"It was on the balcony, taped to the window. She lives on the ninetieth floor. How did someone get a note on the dang balcony?"

Ryder had a few ideas, but he wasn't sharing them with her. He stood up fast, and Gabbi nearly tipped her chair over following suit.

"Take me to Fiona." He was going to straighten this out. Because if he had any hope of protecting Fiona and not letting Flint down, she had to be straightforward with him. She had to let him in so he could do his job.

"You're not supposed to–"

"Now."

As intended, his tone left no room for arguments, and he found himself following Gabbi through the lobby to the elevators. She used a keycard to access the elevators and punched the button for the fifteenth floor.

"She's gonna be so mad at me," Gabbi sang softly to herself.

"You did the right thing," he reassured her.

"I'll be sure to put that in my unemployment paperwork," Gabbi said sarcastically.

He could see Fiona through the window after Gabbi led him down the hallway. She was on the phone, but he didn't care. Despite Gabbi's protests behind him, Ryder pushed open her office door and marched in, shutting Gabbi outside.

Fiona seemed unfazed. "I'm sorry. You'll have to excuse me, but something just came up. Can we finish this when we talk next week? *Grazie.* I'll remember. Thanks, Marvin. *Ciao.*"

Ryder paced the office while he waited. As much as he wanted to explode in frustration, he wouldn't do that. He could restrain himself. Barely.

The moment she hung up, he turned sharply. "What the heck, Fi?"

Calmly, Fiona straightened the pens and papers on her desk, aligning them just so. "Calm down."

"What did the note say?"

"Perhaps you should ask Gabbi," she said with a hint of amusement.

"Don't blame her for this. You should have told me. Then she wouldn't have had to."

"I'll admit, I was a little shaken at first, but I really don't see the big deal."

"A man was on your balcony, Fiona. What if he'd come inside while you were home? What if he hurt Gabbi to get to you?"

———

Fiona's hands stilled. His question cut straight to her core.

"I know you think you're invincible. But you could get hurt. And so could people around you."

The sting of tears behind her eyes had her blinking. "I'm sorry I didn't tell you. I just want this whole situation to go away." She looked at him and saw that his expression had softened. The hard lines of his face filled with frustration and anger only moments ago looked almost… empathetic.

"Have you figured out that this isn't just going away yet?" His tone was quiet, prodding her to continue.

She nodded and exhaled. "I suppose so. I didn't want to believe it was more than just a prank."

"Flint wouldn't send me here over a prank."

A smile played on her lips. "He can be a bit over-protective, you know."

"Maybe. But he was right to be worried this time. Tell me about the note."

"It was there when we got home. You must have missed it during your walk-through or something."

His eyes darkened at the comment and Fiona continued. "It's not your fault or anything. I didn't see it until I was out on the balcony getting some air. It said 'They can't protect you.'"

Ryder swore under his breath. "I can," he said firmly.

Fiona desperately wanted to believe him. "This whole thing is just hard to process."

"You don't have any idea who would want to hurt you?"

She shook her head. "When it was just at the office? Sure. Tons of other food companies or chefs would love to see me take a dive. But I find it hard to believe any of them would actually physically hurt me."

She stood up and walked to the large window that made one wall of the office. She wrapped her arms around herself. Maybe she could hold herself together if she squeezed hard enough.

She spoke to the window, toward the hint of a reflection of Ryder's imposing form still standing across the office. "I don't know, Ryder. People like me. I've built my entire life around never rocking the boat. Never stepping out of line."

She saw his reflection move until Ryder stood just behind her. He laid his hand on her shoulder, and she resisted the urge to lean into the touch.

"Sounds like a lot of pressure," he offered.

She breathed a laugh. "You could say that." How could she adequately explain the feeling of uncertainty and the pressure to be perfect all the time? The looming pressure of everything on her shoulders, afraid she was about to drop one of the dozen balls she was juggling?

When she turned toward him, she saw a look of understanding in his eyes. His eyes searched hers, listening intently as though whatever she had to say was the most important thing in the entire world.

She continued, though she wasn't sure why he made her want to open up. "It could all fall apart so easily. Everything I've built. And this…person…is trying to make that happen. I can't let them. And I won't let them hurt the people close to me."

If they destroyed her business, they destroyed her.

He looked down, his hand sliding down her arm to her fingers before his eyes slid up to hers. "Then let me help you, Fiona. I will stop this guy."

She watched their fingers touch for a moment before Ryder pulled his hand away. A surge of disappointment hit her at the loss of contact. This was Ryder, she reminded herself. She couldn't let herself go there.

She nodded. "Okay."

CHAPTER
SEVEN

IF RYDER HADN'T BEEN THERE himself, he might have thought he imagined the scene with Fiona in her office. In all the years he'd known her brother—and her by extension—he'd never seen Fiona that vulnerable.

She was scared, and he hated that. But at the same time, maybe it was good that the whole situation was finally sinking in. This threat was beginning to feel more real with every passing day.

In fact, he was just about to update Flint. Not a call Ryder was looking forward to, seeing as he was the one who hadn't noticed the note on the balcony window before letting Fiona go into the condo alone.

He'd been kicking himself for it ever since he found out. Still, Flint deserved to know that there had been another threat. And exactly what Ryder was going to do about it. Which meant, he needed to call Miranda before he called Flint.

When she answered, Ryder couldn't help but smile.

"Go for M."

Miranda Bradley was one of the most important parts of their team. Officially, her title was Support and Logistics Officer. In reality, she was the secret key to their success. She made sure that everything went off without a hitch. Vehicles, cameras, and tech were exactly where they needed it—and more importantly, when they needed it.

When she answered, Ryder cut right to the chase. "Hey. You up to speed on my current assignment?"

Miranda answered, "Not really. Flint said you're in New York and to help as needed."

"Perfect. It's a routine bodyguard detail, but things are heating up. I've been staying at a hotel down the street since she's got building security. But apparently that's not enough." It seemed naïve now to think back on that decision. But things had been minor. Until they weren't. "I need something closer. I can't stay in residence, though. Can you see if there is anything available in Pinnacle Heights Tower? Preferably on the top floors. Close to Fiona Raven?"

"Hmmm, that's on West 68th?"

"Affirmative."

Miranda paused. "Let me do some digging. Nothing pops right away."

He frowned at her response. "This is important, M."

"I'm on it. Give me twenty minutes. Anything else?"

He knew Miranda would take care of him. She was quirky and snarky, but she was a magician when it came to making things happen. "That's all. Can you patch me through to Ross?"

"What am I, your secretary?" Her tone was sarcastic, but he heard the line click, and the phone began to ring on the other end of the line.

"Ross McClain."

"Hey, Ross, it's me." It was a strange thing, working for his brother. Ryder knew without a doubt that Ross would have his back. Unfortunately, he knew he didn't provide that same sense of security to the former secret service agent.

"How's the city? Did you grab some pizza yet?"

"No, but I had a bagel the other day that was awesome." Small talk finished, he cut straight to the point. "I wanted to run something past you."

"Sure, what's up?"

"I'm worried about Fiona. I'm doing everything I can to protect her, but I had an idea. Is Andi available to come up here and do a self-defense intensive with Fiona if I can find a time that works? I've never seen someone work so much as Flint's sister, but I think I can make her squeeze something in."

Ross hummed in thought. "I think that could work. I know Andi would be all about it. She's working on some weekly workshops at the local women's shelter, but as long as it wasn't on the same night, I think she'd do it."

"That'd be awesome. I'll get some dates and shoot them to her."

"Sounds good." Ross paused before continuing. "You sure everything's okay?"

"Yeah. I'm working on a few things, and unless she's safely at home or in the office, I don't let Fi out of my sight."

"Fi?"

"Ms. Raven," Ryder corrected. Well, that was smooth.

"Uh-huh." The knowing tone in his brother's voice was irritating.

"Oh, sorry, gotta run. I'll be in touch with Andi. Thanks, Ross."

Ryder hung up the phone with a long exhale. Now

Ross was going to read way more into that than necessary. He could only hope his brother didn't mention anything to Flint.

A text message chimed on his phone.

MB: I've got a line on a place. Need twenty more minutes, but you'll be all set. Floor below Fiona.

RM: Perfect. Thanks, Miranda.

MB: Thank Cole Kensington. Flint called in a favor. It's Cole's place, but he agreed to let you use it.

Ryder lifted his eyebrows. The pharmaceutical CEO was one of Black Tower's routine clients. It was really all about who you knew. What remained to be seen was just how out of place Ryder felt sleeping in the condo of a multi-millionaire. The Bartlett Inn and Suites down the block was fancy enough, and it was just a run-of-the-mill chain hotel. It was all a far cry from the jungles of South America or the back of a jeep in the desert.

————

As tempting as it was to be upset with Gabbi, Fiona couldn't hold a grudge. Especially after her friend insisted on moving in with her until the threat was gone. At first, Ryder had suggested he stay in her guest room, but even the thought of living with him brought heat to her cheeks.

Instead, Ryder would be on the floor below. Knowing he was just a stairwell away was especially reassuring. And having Gabbi there each night was fun, though Fiona missed some of the privacy.

Even Gabbi didn't know about her dress rehearsals for each episode of Rustic Raven, and there was no way to hide the fact that she stayed up until after midnight working just to wake up before sunrise and continue the same.

She'd considered hiding away in her bedroom to work without alerting her friend, but the call of the coffeemaker was too strong. She leaned over her mug and inhaled the rich aroma, feeling the warm air on her face.

A loud yawn jolted her out of the peaceful moment, and she flinched at the sting of hot coffee on the top of her hand. She quickly set the mug down and put a towel to the offending heat. The yawn continued as Gabbi stretched her arms over her head and made her way to the kitchen. Her hot-pink cheetah-print pajama set made Fiona smile. She looked down at her own–navy blue with a delicate white flower pattern. Classic? Or boring?

Gabbi eyed her warily. "Tell me you couldn't

sleep. Because I refuse to believe anyone would wake up this early voluntarily."

Fiona ignored the question. "Did I wake you? I was trying to be quiet."

"Hmph. That dang coffeemaker has a loud beep. Guess I'm a light sleeper."

"Oh. Well, do you want some coffee?"

Gabbi raised her eyebrows at the question. "Does Manhattan smell in the summer?"

Fiona took that as a yes and poured her friend a cup.

After doctoring it up with cream and sugar, Gabbi sat at the counter. "It's not even five o'clock. What are you doing awake anyway?"

Fiona shrugged. "Stuff to do."

"Mmm-hmm. Stuff that can't wait until a reasonable hour?"

"All my reasonable hours are filled with meetings."

Gabbi pulled her cheek to one side. "That's valid."

Fiona sipped her coffee. "There's always so much to do. And then this whole stalker threat and Ryder here… It's a lot."

"I don't know how you do it." Gabbi looked around. "Well, apparently by getting far less sleep than the average person needs. But you know you don't have to do it all, right? You've got an entire team of people that could help you!"

She considered her friend's words. It wasn't that she hadn't thought about it. It was just that she needed to make sure everything was done to her standards. And that meant putting her own eyes on it at the very least, if not simply doing it herself. Even if it meant running on five hours of sleep a night.

"I'm okay, Gab. Really."

"You keep telling yourself that, Fi. I don't buy it. And neither does Ryder, for the record." Gabbi gave her a mischievous smile. "Your brother sure knows how to pick 'em. That man is fine!"

Fiona nearly spit out her coffee. "Gabbi!"

"What? I didn't realize lack of sleep made you blind."

"He's just a friend," she insisted. "Besides, he's here to protect me. Nothing more."

She couldn't fault Gabbi's evaluation, though. Ryder was definitely good-looking. But more than that, he was…intense. She was beginning to realize that his bad boy vibe wasn't all good-natured pranks. The more time she spent with him, the more she saw mysterious depths within him. Hints of his past dropped in conversation, tinged with regret.

And when he listened to her, Fiona felt like there was nothing in the world that could turn his attention away from her. He approached everything with a single-minded focus few people seemed to have. And right now, all that energy was focused on one thing.

Her.

It was honestly a bit intimidating. And far too tempting.

"I'm just saying…"

"Yeah, yeah. I hear you just saying…" Fiona grabbed her coffee cup and headed back to her room. "I'm taking a shower. We leave at six!"

CHAPTER EIGHT

FIONA FROWNED at the sight of police cars outside the Raven Foods offices. She glanced at her phone for the first time since leaving home. Three missed calls and a voicemail from Daniels.

Usually, she spent the car ride to work answering emails or running through menus. But with Gabbi and Ryder in the car as well, she'd been preoccupied with the conversation.

Ryder climbed out of the car, then held a hand up to stop her. "Wait here until I check it out."

She was tempted to roll her eyes, but held it back. Instead, she clicked on the voicemail.

"It's Jim. We've had a break-in at the offices." She made eye contact with Gabbi as the message continued loud enough for them each to hear.

"Everyone is safe. As far as I can tell, the building is clear and they're long gone. More info when you get here."

No longer waiting for Ryder to come back, Fiona opened the door and stepped out. In case anyone was watching, she strode confidently into the building, letting her knee-length pea coat blow in the wind.

Perhaps if she acted like nothing was wrong, it would be so.

In the lobby, she found Ryder, Jim, and one of NYPD's finest in a circle. She turned to Gabbi. "Go upstairs and get started on the day. I'll be up soon."

Gabbi nodded and Fiona veered toward the trio while Gabbi headed for the elevator.

"I thought I told you to stay in the car."

She ignored Ryder's comment and held out her hand to the officer. "I'm Fiona Raven. Can you tell me what happened?"

The officer shook her hand and stood up straight. "Officer Perkins. Ms. Raven, I'm afraid there isn't much the NYPD can do for you. Mr. Daniels here has shown me the security footage—well, the lack thereof."

She turned to Jim with an expectant look.

He shook his head. "They spoofed the connection on every camera they might have been spotted on. By the time we realized there was a break-in, they could have been gone for hours. Best we can tell, they were here between three and four this morning."

"And our team saw nothing?"

"Sorry."

She swallowed her frustration. It wouldn't do to be emotional and cause a scene. Never cause a scene.

"What did they take?"

Jim answered her with a frustrated tone. "That's the thing, Miss Raven. We can't tell. They hit a records room. Trashed it, in fact. If there is something missing, it could take us weeks to figure out what it was."

The officer pulled out a notepad. "We'll file a report, but it sounds like this is mostly a corporate security concern."

"Perkins, there's more–" Ryder started to say, but the NYPD officer cut him off.

"If I remember correctly, Mr. McClain, you might not be the best judge of what is truly a matter for further investigation. I don't believe I'll be taking your advice."

She had no idea what he was talking about, but Ryder's face immediately changed. He was undoubtedly furious at the brush-off.

"Don't punish her because you don't like me. There have been other—"

"Thank you, officer. We appreciate your time." She gave Ryder a look she hoped he would be able to interpret. They had no way of knowing if this was related to her stalker. It could just be a disgruntled employee or something. And whatever history he had with Officer Perkins was not helping.

When Perkins had gone, Fiona turned back to her team. "Get to the bottom of this. I'll follow up later today." She turned to the elevator and took a few steps. Then, she turned back. "And find out what files are missing."

She left Daniels and Ryder there to confer. She had things to do. And she wasn't letting some two-bit thief derail her day. Stalker or no, Daniels had said he was long gone.

Which should have been reassuring, but her hands still shook as she reached for the elevator button.

———

Ryder snapped photos of the destroyed file room with his phone. The thief had covered their tracks by essentially tossing the contents of every file cabinet across the small room.

But why? With their ability to bypass the security feeds, they could have snuck in, grabbed what they were looking for, and made a clean exit.

If they even took anything, this was also about messing with Fiona. Otherwise, it would have been done quietly. They wanted her–and him–to know what they could do. That they could go places they shouldn't be able to go. Just like they had the morning they went to Gabbi's desk and placed a note there. Just to prove they could.

Ryder smacked the side of a file cabinet with his hand in frustration. He'd been here for two weeks and he'd done nothing that was getting him any closer to eliminating the threat against Fiona. All he'd done was ride in a car with her to and from work and camp out in the lobby of her building.

Now, he was sleeping in the apartment below hers. And after this little incident? He was going to be her shadow, even at work. He wasn't taking no for an answer.

And he was going to get to the bottom of this threat. Even if the NYPD refused to help. No surprise there. One look at Ryder and Perkins had decided this was another case of The Boy Who Cried Wolf.

"Do we have any idea what was taken?" he asked Daniels, who was standing at the doorway to the file room. Joey's background check on the head of security had come back clean, as expected.

Daniels shook his head. "There's an inventory of what is in the room. But it'll take weeks to cross reference that with what is still here. If it's even accurate."

"I'm going to need a copy of that inventory." He'd send it to Joey, see if she could flag anything that might be a potential target.

"Sure. I'll send it over. And I'll work on getting someone assigned to sort through this."

Ryder nodded at Daniels. "Appreciate it. If we're going to figure this out, we can't waste any time." He headed for the door. "I'm going to go see Fio—Ms. Raven. I'll touch base later."

He took the elevator to the fifteenth floor and followed the familiar hallway toward Fiona's office. To his surprise, Gabbi didn't stop him, and Fiona waved him in, despite the phone to her ear.

"It's good to talk to you, too. I can't wait to hear your vision for the Valentine's edition of *Date Night America*. I've got tons of ideas, but I want to make sure we're going in the same direction." She tucked her hair behind her ear and laughed. "Of course it is. I'll see you soon. *Ciao.*"

If he didn't already know, he wouldn't be able to

tell that anything unusual had happened this morning. Her voice, her laugh…all of it was completely unaffected.

She hung up the phone, and just for a moment, he thought he saw her composure slip. It was just a blip, and then she turned to him, eyes bright and cheerful.

"What do you have, Mr. McClain?"

He raised an eyebrow at the formality but responded anyway. "We've got a major security risk with a personal vendetta against you, *Ms. Raven.*" Two could play at that game. "I'm changing the game plan. From now on, I will be your escort at all times when not safely at your home."

Her mouth fell open. "Absolutely not."

"It wasn't a question. Our guy keeps escalating. And he has now proven twice that not only can he beat your security system–which Flint has assured me is no easy task, seeing as it is from Raven Security–he isn't afraid to infiltrate not only the lower floors in the middle of the night, but the fifteenth floor during the middle of the work day."

She sagged slightly and he stepped closer, sensing her resolve weakening. "Fiona. I just want to keep you safe. And I need to be close to you to do that."

Fiona paused and pressed her lips together. "What does he want?"

He shook his head. "I don't know. I was going to ask you the same thing. What could have been in that storage room that he wanted?"

"There's nothing in there except corporate finance and research documents. Some manufacturing records... Nothing exciting."

"They thought something in there was important enough to steal. I'm working another angle, but if you can think of anything, let me know."

"I will."

"Good." He looked around her office at the sparse furnishings. "Now, tell me where I should sit."

FIONA GLANCED up at the rhythmic vibration. Ryder's knee bounced up and down, the motion shaking the floor just enough to be felt in the otherwise silent office.

"Can you not?"

"Huh?" Ryder looked up at her with confusion.

She gave a pointed glance toward his knee. The movement ceased, and she exhaled a deep sigh. "Thank you," she said.

Ryder had been camped in her office for the last three days. Not just her office, but he had sat in the corner of every conference call, board meeting, and one-on-one chat with staff members. He stood—or sat —like a shadow she couldn't shake.

Except for when he wasn't a statue. The man

fidgeted. And after three days of it, Fiona had hit her breaking point.

She wasn't sure, but there was a chance it wasn't the fidgeting that bugged her. Every time she almost forgot he was there, Ryder would clear his throat, shift in his chair, or sometimes she simply felt his eyes watching her.

To be honest, she hadn't gotten any significant amount of work done in the last three days.

"Is there any chance you could guard me from outside in the hallway?"

Ryder was already shaking his head when she finished the question. "That is not an option. They made it to your balcony. There is nothing stopping them from reaching your office from the outside. I stay in here, princess."

Fiona pushed down the frustration. She knew he was right, but that didn't make it any easier for him to be there. In her space. All day. Every day. And if he called her princess one more time… She exhaled to regain her composure.

"Fine." She stood up to get a bottle of water.

"What are you working on?"

Fiona looked back at her desk. From his perspective, he could only see the back of her computer and a few stacks of papers.

"I'm reviewing December's financials. Manufacturing, show ratings, et cetera."

The numbers had just been finalized for the
previous year. And it had been a good one. December
was always a good month for sales in her manufactured foods division, but a down month for production. Inventory was the lowest it would be all year.
Her frozen pies and casseroles helped some people
make it through the holidays.

"Why don't you let someone else handle that
entire side of the business? Wouldn't it be easier if
you could just be on camera and in the kitchen?"

It wasn't the first time Fiona had been asked that
question. Still, she considered her words carefully as
she leaned against the counter and took a drink.

"It's true that I got into this business first and
foremost because I loved to cook. But the truth is, I
also love the challenge of running a business. All of
the pieces that fit together to create a product and
deliver it to people around the country. It is
fascinating."

Ryder hummed. She couldn't help but wonder
what he thought of her.

"Why do you ask?"

He shrugged. "I don't know. It just seems like a
lot for one person. And you seem to put more pres-

sure on yourself than anyone I've ever met. And I've met some very important people. Even if I don't include Ross or Flint, which I typically don't."

She gave a slight smile. "I know the feeling. Sometimes, I forget that Flint was the inventor and CEO of a multi-billion dollar company. I forget that he has more understanding of my life than most other people. He has been in similar shoes. I mean, Raven Foods is a drop in the bucket compared to Raven Tech."

"He's changed," Ryder said. "Since your mom died, that is."

Fiona nodded. "We both did. It took Mom's death for Flint to realize what was important to him."

"And you?"

She turned her back on him and made her way back to her desk, blinking back the tears that threatened. "I only ever wanted to make my parents proud. So that's what I'm doing." Losing her mother had been hard. And her father a few years later? Devastating.

She knew that her desire to gain her parents' approval was something that drove her toward success. That wasn't a bad thing, right? Growing up, it had seemed that approval was never forthcoming. There had always been something to change or fix.

When he spoke again, he was closer. "They would be proud."

She turned to find him only feet away, across the desk. She nodded and swallowed through the lump in her throat at his words. He looked at her with such admiration. But if he knew her more, would he see the same flaws her mother had?

She didn't want to entertain the question. Changing the subject was safer. "What about you? You were NYPD, right? Then it was like you fell off the map. What happened?"

———

Ryder took a seat in one of the chairs directly across from Fiona's desk. How much was he willing to tell her?

"It's a long story," he said. "Suffice it to say, I lost my position with the department. The truth is, I'm nobody's hero."

"I don't believe that. You're here. You work for Flint. That means something, doesn't it?"

"All it means is that the good people in my life aren't willing to give up on me. Which I guess is a blessing." He shrugged. "It would be easier for them if they did."

Fiona shook her head. "I don't believe that. They love you. And they see something in you."

He scoffed. "Yeah, maybe so. I keep trying to be the man they think I am."

That was exactly what had gotten him into the situation. Out of his depth, protecting Fiona from a threat that was as slippery as the noodles in her *fettuccine al forno.*

Sitting here in her office or following her to meetings—all of it felt like he was just waiting for the next shoe to drop.

Fiona walked around her desk and sat against the edge of it. She was mere inches away. If he wanted to, he could reach out and touch her. Instead, he dug his fingers into his thighs.

"Well, from what I have seen, you are the man they think you are."

Ryder let her words of approval sink into his soul. Maybe if she believed it, he could believe it too. As he was debating how to respond, his phone buzzed in his pocket. He pulled it out to find a file from Joey. He glanced up at Fiona. "You got a minute?"

He ran through the list that Joey had sent of potentially targeted files from the records room. "Based on your list of inventory, these are the files Joey suspects someone might have been interested in taking. Do any of these sound familiar, or trip anything for you?"

He handed Fiona the phone and she read the list. "Why would anyone be interested in my old failed research? Or legal records from Chicago a decade ago?"

"I don't know, corporate espionage? Maybe you missed something they think they can use."

She shook her head. "Your guess is as good as mine."

Considering his guess was nonexistent, that was less than helpful.

"I'll just hang on to this list. Maybe it will make sense later."

And once again, he had nothing to go on. The only thing he could do was stay close to Fiona. Not exactly a hardship, but the threat was still looming over them.

"You'll find him," she said.

He met her eyes, momentarily allowing himself to be lost in the dark-brown depths. He wanted to believe her.

———

Fiona mentally recited the script that went along with the dish she was making. Usually, she would say it out loud. But Ryder sat across the counter in her kitchen, making her even more nervous than he'd been making her for the last week as he sat in her office.

Gabbi was busy tonight, which meant Ryder was babysitting.

Her words, not his.

She closed her eyes and tried to remember what she was supposed to talk about while she browned the pancetta. Was it the info about bacon compared to pancetta? Or was that later, when she added it to the pasta?

"Something wrong, princess?"

Her eyes flew open at his voice. The way her heart quivered when he called her princess was disconcerting. Somehow, there was no acid in the insult. But it had to be an insult, didn't it? "No. Just thinking."

"What's with the feast? You already fixed salmon, right? I promise I'm not picky."

She smiled. "I know you aren't. I see you eat a ham and cheese sandwich almost every day for lunch, remember?"

He flushed. "Oh yeah. What can I say? I'm a simple man."

She stirred the pancetta. "Well, this baked lemon ziti goes fantastic with fish."

He grabbed one of the stuffed mushrooms she'd already prepped. "And these?"

She shrugged. "Sounded good?"

He popped one in his mouth and chewed. "Mmm, they are that. But I'm not buying it. You don't like me enough to fix a three-course dinner just because."

"Gabbi never asks this many questions when I cook for her," she said, pointing the spoon at him.

He laughed. "Doesn't changed the fact that I *am* asking."

She sighed. "Fine. I'm just doing a run-through of one of the upcoming episodes we're taping. Making sure I remember the recipes. And what I'm supposed to say."

He grabbed another mushroom. "It seems like maybe this rehearsal would be more effective if you were actually speaking the words you need to remember."

She raised her eyebrows. "And it seems like maybe you're going to talk your way right out of a home-cooked dinner."

His face cracked into a wide grin at her threat, and

she burst into laughter. "Stop making me laugh, Mac!"

She froze at the words, and she saw his smile slip. Why was it she was always telling him to stop? Fiona had more fun with Ryder McClain that she did anyone else on the planet, with the possible exception of Gabbi. But just like with Gabbi, it came easily with Ryder.

Until she put an end to it.

Like she always did.

Like she was expected to.

She slipped into her Rustic Raven voice and spoke to the microwave above her stove. "Now, if you can't find pancetta, you can always use bacon. I recommend blanching it in boiling water before you brown it up to remove some of the smoky flavor, if you want a flavor closer to traditional pancetta."

She glanced back at Ryder at the counter. Did he think she was ridiculous for this extra rehearsal?

"But what if I like the smoky flavor?"

A smile teased her lips again at his playful question. "As much as science plays a part, cooking is still an art. And you get to be the artist."

He pointed at himself, then looked over his shoulder before looking back at her. "Me?"

She giggled. "Yes, you. Ham and cheese sandwich addiction aside, you could learn to cook."

He stood up and made his way into the kitchen. "Okay. Teach me."

Her eyes widened. If having Ryder watching her from across the room was nerve-racking, having him inside the kitchen was positively anxiety inducing.

She turned back to the stove and stirred the pancetta, wincing when she saw the dark-brown edges. "Rats!" she scolded herself for forgetting it.

"What's wrong?"

"I burned the pancetta!" Distracted by Ryder, no doubt. She pulled the pan off the heat and took a deep breath.

He leaned in. "Looks okay to me," he offered with a shrug.

"It's not," she said firmly. An error like this on set would mean redoing the entire segment. And probably whispers about her skills among the crew. Unacceptable.

"Do you want me to go back and sit down?" He rested one hip on the edge of the counter, the gentle expression in his eyes easing the sting of her mistake.

"No… You should stay." She groped for a job to give him. What was she cooking again? "Check the water and see if it's boiling."

He lifted the lid. "Not quite." He replaced the lid and turned back to her. "You know… Sometimes, mistakes happen. No one would judge you for it."

She exhaled. "They would. Which is why I make them here instead of in front of other people. Bad enough that you saw it."

She felt his eyes on her as she spooned the pancetta out of the pan.

"People might surprise you," he said quietly. Then, he checked the water again. "Looks like it's boiling now."

About ten minutes later, Fiona had successfully coached Ryder through creating the sauce for the lemon ziti. Fully relaxed, she now occupied his previous spot on the counter and directed him as she sipped her drink. "Now just dump all of those into a casserole dish and toss it in the oven, along with the salmon."

His forearms flexed as he lifted the mixing bowl and spooned the pasta into the dish. Her eyes were drawn to the movement, and she took another drink.

Her eyebrows flew upward as he grabbed the breadcrumbs already on the counter, mixed them with the parmesan cheese and added some Italian herbs without instruction. Then, he spread it on the casserole before slipping it in the oven.

She waited until he turned back to her before giving him a raise-eyebrow look of accusation. "What was that?"

His eyes darted back and forth in an exaggerated look of innocence. "Who, me?"

"You can cook?"

He smiled sheepishly. "I know a few things. But it was more fun to have you teach me," he said with a wink.

Fiona felt herself blush, remembering how she'd used the excuse of showing him how to make a roux to get close, brushing up against him as he stirred the flour and butter mixture. She buried her face in her hands.

The man was incorrigible.

But also…She hadn't laughed so much while cooking for a long time. She hadn't even realized that some of the joy had been missing.

CHAPTER
TEN

RYDER KEPT one eye on Gabbi and one eye on the surroundings. Being out like this made him remember why he hated New York. Protective detail here was impossible, unless you had the resources of the Secret Service.

Strangers passed by in the opposite direction. People came out of office buildings and restaurants as they walked past. Ryder scanned for anything out of the ordinary. Then he scanned again. A gust of wind pushed against him. The short two-block walk definitely felt longer with the winter wind whipping down the sidewalk. He pulled his hat farther down over his ears and tucked his hands in the pockets of his jacket.

Gabbi lifted her shoulders to bring her scarf

farther around her neck and ears as they walked back to the office. "Brrr." She shivered. "I'm ready for spring!"

"Me too. But not until after Valentine's Day," Fiona said with a laugh.

"Forget Valentine's Day. Other than your prime-time special, I'm all about Galentine's Day this year —brunch with my ladies because we don't need a man! What about you, Mac? Got a valentine in mind?"

He raised an eyebrow but didn't answer. Like he had the entire outing, Ryder kept his eyes moving, watching everything around them. Gabbi was a few steps ahead, walking briskly and turning around to talk to them every few steps. He kept Fiona close. Just in case.

Gabbi was still talking. She was *always* talking. "Almost there. Do we have a fireplace in the office? We should get a fireplace!"

Fiona chuckled. She responded to Gabbi, but something made him turn, and her words faded into a roar in his ears.

A white passenger van veered toward them. The rear axle was already jumping the curb. Ryder ripped his hands from his pockets, reaching desperately for

Fiona's elbow. He pushed her to the side, wrapping his arms around her as he tackled her out of the way of the van. They tumbled to the ground and he cushioned her fall with his own body. As the van passed them, the tires skidded on the pavement next to them. He shouted a warning to Gabbi. It was too late. He shielded Fiona from the view. There was as sickening thud as the van clipped Gabbi.

Other pedestrians jumped out of the way. Their screams melded with the squeal of tires as the van returned to the street and sped off. He rose to his feet and chased the van for a few steps, but it was hopeless. They were gone.

"Gabbi!" The hoarse cry came from Fiona, pushing up from the sidewalk where he'd left her.

He grabbed his cellphone and frantically dialed 911 as he ran toward Fiona and Gabbi. "A van hit a pedestrian. We need an ambulance!" He hurriedly gave them the cross streets. The operator kept talking, but he hung up.

Fiona was sobbing, screaming at the sight of her friend lying like a ragdoll on the sidewalk. Fiona's wail cut through his heart. He pulled her back gently, then waited until she had quieted enough to hear him. He pointed at the Raven Foods offices only thirty yards away. They'd been so close to the safety of a building.

"Go inside. Find Daniels!"

Fiona looked back at Gabbi, tears streaked down her face. Sniffling, she looked back at him, questioning.

"I've got her. I need you to run."

She took a shaky breath and nodded. As he'd hoped, the task seemed to focus her.

He knelt over Gabbi, keeping one eye on Fiona's figure jogging toward the entrance. He assessed her injuries. Most concerning was the blood pooling under her head. Praying it wasn't serious, he looked further. A broken leg. That was obvious from the grotesque angle of her thigh. He felt her neck, relieved to find a pulse beating strongly under his fingers. He resisted the urge to move her.

The moments stretched on. Where was that ambulance? She began moaning and he shushed her. "It's going to be okay. You're okay, Gabbi."

The ambulance pulled up on the curb and two paramedics jumped out in dark blue. "Step back, sir."

He stood and moved away as he spoke to them. "A van jumped the curb and the front corner hit her. She hit her head on the sidewalk."

The paramedics took care to stabilize her neck

and splint her leg. Still, as they lifted her onto the stretcher, Gabbi cried out.

Fiona came up beside him, panting. He turned to see Jim Daniels followed close behind. "What did they say?"

"Nothing yet."

While the paramedics worked, the police had arrived and set up a basic perimeter around the scene. Bystanders were watching with morbid curiosity. He wanted to yell at them to go away. Was it fun to watch a woman bleed out on the sidewalk? What was wrong with people?

"Sir, I'm going to need you all to step back."

Ryder turned to see a uniformed police officer gesturing them away from Gabbi.

"Cheno, is that you?" Tim Chenoweth had been one of his closer friends in the department. Not that it was worth much these days.

The officer's eyes narrowed. "Mac?"

Ryder's tension faded and he smiled tightly. He could use an ally, but he doubted one would come from within the NYPD. "It's been ages."

"Sure has." Cheno looked over his shoulder at Gabbi being loaded into the ambulance. "She a friend of yours?"

He nodded solemnly.

"You see what happened?"

"Yeah." He relayed the events to Officer Chenoweth.

"Listen, I need that footage," he said frankly.

Cheno thought about it. "I'll see what I can do, Mac. Since it's you."

Ryder hid his surprise. That was the last thing he expected. "Thanks. I appreciate it."

"Not at all. If you need anything else while you're in the city, you know how to get a hold of me."

Was it possible that not every relationship from his former life had been damaged beyond repair? He looked at Cheno's eyes, but he couldn't tell. It seemed too good to be true, but he needed the assist. Ryder clapped a hand on Cheno's shoulder. "I owe you, man."

He heard Fiona yelling behind him. She was trying to climb into the ambulance, while the EMT was blocking her way.

He shook his head. "I'm sorry, ma'am. This isn't TV. No passengers."

Ryder said her name to get her attention as she argued with him. "We'll meet her there. Come with me."

Fiona looked back and forth from her friend to him and shook her head. "No. I'm going with her."

The EMT who was already inside the ambulance yelled, "She's losing a lot of blood! We need to move!"

The driver nodded and shut the door. Fiona looked back at him, the helpless expression on her face breaking his heart.

CHAPTER
ELEVEN

FIONA RAN her fingers over the row of buttons on her blazer. Up and down the perfectly spaced line of pearl circles. The feel of the fabric and the hard decorations were the only thing that grounded her in this moment. Otherwise, she felt like she might float away.

They descended into the dark shadows of the hospital parking garage, turning left and right through the maze of rows. And she prayed. Desperate pleas of mercy and healing for her friend. She'd lost people before. Her mother had been the most painful of all. But she hadn't known about the attack in Nashville until after it had happened. Gabbi's unknown fate was excruciating. She was on a tightrope of emotion, not knowing which way the wind would blow. Would she walk into the hospital just to be told her friend was gone?

The car stopped as Ryder pulled into a parking space and killed the engine. And then it was silent. Everything seemed eerily still after the deluge of chaos that had been the incident on the street. Screams and sirens would haunt her dreams tonight.

She kept reliving the moment it happened. Ryder's hand jerking her elbow and shoving her out of the way, then crashing to the ground in Ryder's protective arms. If he hadn't pushed her, the van would have hit her head on. Would that have saved Gabbi? She hung her head in her hands. Whoever had driven that van was aiming for her. She knew that, but Gabbi had paid the price. If the looming weight of these threats hadn't been enough over the past few weeks, they certainly seemed crushing now.

"Come on, let's go inside and wait." Ryder walked around the car and held out a hand to help her out. The elevator ride to the lobby took an eternity, but Fiona had slipped her hand back into his once the doors slid closed. Fiona leaned into him, letting him be her strength for this moment. He let her hand go as they went inside, tucking her gently under his arm as they made their way to the waiting room.

Later, she could stand tall as she addressed the

rest of her staff. But for now, with the fate of Gabbi still in the hands of God and the doctors? She couldn't seem to bear the weight alone.

"I can't lose Gabbi." The words in no way expressed how desperately she needed her friend to be okay. Gabbi was an anchor for her. Without her, Fiona was afraid she might just drift. She needed Gabbi to be okay. And she would do anything to make sure that was the case.

Right now, she was just helpless. And she hated that feeling.

————

Daytime talk shows droned on from the waiting room television. Ryder realized his knee was bouncing and stopped it with a quick glance at Fiona. She wasn't paying any attention to him. She looked…lost.

He turned over the thoughts that had been chasing him since the lobby. It seemed like no matter what he did, he was bound to let Fiona down. Gabbi being hurt had obviously shaken her. He thought she'd been rattled with the note on the balcony or the records room. But he'd never seen her like this.

She stared blankly at a spot on the floor in front of

the check-in desk. Just like she had been for the last twenty minutes.

"Are you okay, Fi?"

Still staring, she shook her head. "No."

Unsure of what to do, he wrapped an arm around her. "She's going to be okay."

"You don't know that!" Fiona's voice cracked on the words.

"She's in the best hands. And Gabbi's a fighter. She's probably in there right now cracking a joke about how the doctor doesn't look enough like McDreamy."

Fiona laughed and sniffled. "How do you even know about McDreamy? Are you a *Grey's Anatomy* fan?"

He smiled, grateful that he'd managed to break through her shock. "I can neither confirm nor deny that accusation."

She chuckled, but the sound drifted away as the moment faded. "Thanks," she whispered.

"Is there someone we need to call? Gabbi's family?" Back at the scene, giving Fiona something to do had brought her out of her shock. He was groping for something like that again.

Fiona shook her head. "No. Her mom kicked her out when she was a teenager. Her dad was never in the picture. I'm her family. I'm even her emergency contact." Fiona sounded distraught at the fact. "I'm all she has. And she's hurt because of me!"

"Shh, it's okay. This isn't your fault." He rubbed her arm. "First things first. Do you have something you can give to the hospital so they'll give you info on her condition?"

Fiona thought about it for a moment, then her eyes lit up. "Yes! I've got a copy of the POA somewhere. I'll just call Ashley and have her find it."

"That's good. Hopefully, she'll be able to tell them herself soon, but until then, at least they can keep you updated."

Revived by the prospect of accomplishing something, Fiona stood and started making calls. Her forlorn look was replaced by resolve as she issued orders.

Ryder picked up the phone and called Flint.

"What's going on?"

"You'll probably see it on the news soon, so I wanted to call you myself." Ryder took a deep breath. "There was an incident outside Fiona's office."

"What happened?"

"Someone tried to run us down in a utility van. I got Fiona out of the way, but her assistant, Gabbi, was hit. She's at the hospital, in surgery now."

"I'm sending a team." Ryder wasn't sure whether to sigh in relief or argue that it wasn't necessary. But before he could, Flint swore under his breath. "I can't. Everybody is tied up on this rescue job down in Mexico." He paused. "I'll see if Andi can come."

"You don't have to do that. I won't let Fiona out of my sight." He watched her even then, across the waiting room as she paced while on the phone.

"If she's available, she's coming. But our mission will be executed in ninety-six hours, and, God willing, the hostages safely delivered in three days. Once everyone is back stateside, I'm sending Tank and Marshall to you."

Flint's tone left no room for argument. Not that Ryder wanted to argue.

"Roger that." He shouldn't be surprised. It was only a matter of time before Flint realized that he'd been wrong to trust Ryder.

Flint's voice was less commanding when he spoke again. "You are still the lead on this. It doesn't mean you have to do it alone."

Ryder shook his head. "You'd be better off putting Tank in charge."

"No way. Take care of my sister. We'll be there in eight days."

Fiona scheduled a corporate-wide staff meeting for the next day, followed shortly after by a press conference. After drafting a statement, she zipped through emails, delegating absolutely everything she could to the various directors who reported to her. Perhaps this was her chance to realize she didn't have to do everything herself.

Each time she looked up from her work at the dreary waiting room, she prayed again for Gabbi. Prayer didn't feel like enough, though she believed in the power of it.

She couldn't help but feel overwhelmed by guilt. The monster who was targeting Fiona had gone too far. What did she need to do to end this? Because she would do it. She was ready to do anything to make it stop.

She was tired of living her life in hiding. She'd been avoiding restaurants and events. Today was the one day she'd convinced Ryder and Gabbi to grab lunch at the deli down the street, and look what happened. She couldn't live like this forever. And she'd never forgive herself for putting Gabbi in danger.

A new email came in and she frowned at the subject line. **Scandal shuts down Raven Foods.**

She clicked on the email and the images loaded. How had this made it past the spam filters?

The email itself made her stomach wretch. If she'd managed to eat anything in the last eight hours, she was sure she would have lost it. The words on the document were unfamiliar. But it was her signature at the bottom, dated nearly ten years ago when Raven Foods was just a small start-up in the manufactured foods sector.

Eight identical documents, with only the name and numbers changed.

"While Raven Foods, Inc. maintains the position that no error in manufacturing or lapse in safety measures caused the illness in Chase Meyers, Raven Foods, Inc. offers the following compensation, as a sign of good faith and our deepest sympathies for your loss."

The letter went on to offer the family a settlement in exchange for an ironclad Non-Disclosure Agreement. She remembered the scare. But she distinctly remembered being assured by the $500 per hour law firm–recommended by Flint–that it was nothing to be concerned about. In fact, it was one reason she maintained such a close chain of communication with the manufacturing segment. She was determined to never let anything like it happen again.

A few people had been sick, but it hadn't been her fault. Or at least, that's what she thought. That's what the lawyers had told her. She'd been so busy dealing with her mom's death and trying to stay on top of her business, she'd trusted them.

And they'd turned around and offered each family a generous settlement to shut them up. She was going to be sick. How had she missed this?

At the bottom of the email, she saw familiar bold letters.

$50,000 cash or the dark past of Raven Foods is on the six o'clock news and Miss Lindsey never sees the outside of that hospital.

Ditch the shadow and go to Times Square Stairs at 1145pm. We'll call with more instructions.

Fiona's heart dropped. She couldn't let them hurt Gabbi any more than they already had.

And even if she could somehow protect her friend, if word of this incident got out, her entire company could be destroyed. The lawyers might have made sure she couldn't be taken to court, but she knew very well that the court of public opinion wasn't nearly so picky about the evidence.

The crushing weight of failure settled on her shoulders. She'd been young and more careless than she was now, but she should have known. Not paying closer attention was a mistake of gigantic proportions. And it never should have happened.

She prided herself on her honesty. But also, she dreaded the thought of how her friends would look at her when they found out she'd covered up this incident. Surely, Ryder's flirtatious touches and admiring glances would disappear when she wasn't a perfect "princess" anymore.

Fiona was preoccupied when she finally got to see Gabbi later that day. She built it up so much in her mind, expecting the worst, that she was surprised how normal Gabbi looked. Her leg was in a cast, and there were bruises and scrapes on her arms and face. Otherwise, she was peaceful in sleep.

Fiona held Gabbi's hand and her heart cried desperate, wordless prayers. Tears streamed down her face, and for the first time in ages, Fiona wasn't the least bit concerned about who could see.

As she watched, Gabbi rolled her head over to look at Fiona. Her voice was rough and labored. "I'm filing workman's comp."

Leave it to Gab to crack a joke from the hospital bed.

Fiona laughed through the tears and nodded. "Anything, Gab. I'll take care of it all. I'm so, so sorry."

"Not…fault." Then Gabbi dozed off again.

Fiona got the message. Gabbi didn't blame her. But that wouldn't stop her from blaming herself. If it hadn't been for her mistakes, this person would never have been after her. And if they hadn't been targeting Fiona, Gabbi would never have been in the crosshairs.

The nurse came in, logging into the computer at Gabbi's bedside. "Are you…" She checked the notes. "Fiona Raven?"

Fiona nodded. "Your friend here has suffered quite the trauma. I'm going to grab her vitals and then I'll give you an update, okay?" Fiona held her friend's hand through the conversation. A broken leg, two cracked ribs, and a concussion.

Tears filled her eyes as she realized how long the road to recovery would be. And it was all her fault.

She stepped out of the room and found Ryder waiting patiently outside.

"She's asleep. But they said she's going to be okay."

He nodded. "What do you need to do?"

She needed to go back in time and fix her mistakes from ten years ago. But instead, she said, "I need to run to the office, but only for an hour. Then I want to come back."

One hour at the office quickly turned into three. Fiona brought her dinner with her when she went back to see Gabbi again.

"About time you showed up," Gabbi greeted her.

Fiona raised an eyebrow and returned one sarcastic comment with another. "You know, if you wanted to have dinner with me, you could've just asked. Getting run over was a bit of overkill."

Gabbi's chuckle turned into a groan.

Fiona winced. "How's the pain? Should I call the nurse?"

"No, no. I'm okay. Just don't make me laugh."

Fiona used the remote to put the hospital bed into a seated position. While they ate together, Gabbi complained about the bland hospital food and Fiona shared her Chinese food. Afterward, she saw Gabbi fighting to keep her eyes open. "Here, let me get you settled in for the night."

She lowered the bed and repositioned the pillows. She reached gingerly for her friend's hand. "I'm so sorry, Gab."

If all these people wanted was money, why go after her friend? Was it really just to scare her and make a point? Mission accomplished.

Gabbi shook her head sleepily. "Not your fault."

Fiona shook her head. "It is my fault. They did this because of me. Because I screwed up."

"You never screw up," her friend said adamantly, more awake now.

Fiona felt her control slipping. She knew what she had to do. The stalker could come after her, and he could come after her business. But she wouldn't let him come after her friends. If she could get him off her back with a cash payment, she'd do it.

Then, maybe her life could go back to normal. She would have Ryder take her home and then she could sneak out while he thought she was sleeping. This way, even Ryder didn't have to know. Then maybe he would continue looking at her like she was the most beautiful thing he'd ever seen. And Gabbi would be safe.

Gabbi looked at her with such trust. "I did. I'm so sorry. Please don't hate me. I'm going to fix this. They just want money. I'm going to go tonight and pay them and then we'll all be safe."

Gabbi struggled to sit up, then gave up with a huff. "You can't do this."

Fiona shushed her and glanced at the door where Ryder was waiting outside. "Shhh. Yes, I can." If she didn't, they'd kill Gabbi. And they'd expose everything.

"Fi, listen to me."

Fiona paused her pacing and Gabbi continued. "This isn't your fault. And even if you somehow made a mistake, it's okay. I know it's hard to believe, but nobody's perfect. And I love you no matter what."

Fiona heard the words of her friend, but the bandages and beeping made it difficult to believe. This was her fault. And losing her friend or her company because of her mistake wasn't an option. "I'm sorry, Gab. I have to do this."

Before Gabbi could talk her out of it, Fiona said good night and hastily made her exit. With her friend stable and someone from Raven Foods security posted outside the room all night, Fiona needed to work on the next part of her plan.

CHAPTER
TWELVE

RYDER SET the bag of leftover takeout down on the floor outside the condo and went in to clear the space. Gun drawn, he quickly checked each room and closet—and the balcony—before giving Fiona the all clear to come in.

"Thanks, Ryder. I'm glad you were with me today."

He looked at her and she tried not to squirm. Clearing his throat, he said, "It's my job. But, Fi, I've got your back. I'm sorry I didn't have Gabbi's too."

She nodded. "It's not your fault."

"Not yours either."

She yawned and looked back at the door. "You want to take your food downstairs or what? I'm probably just going to crash." Ryder had said he wasn't hungry earlier when she ate with Gabbi.

Ryder pulled the Styrofoam containers out of the bag and began searching for plates and utensils. "That's fine. I'm staying here tonight, anyway."

Her deer in the headlights look made it clear that she wasn't exactly thrilled by the proposition.

"Don't worry, I already cleared it with Flint. Since Gabbi's going to be out of commission for a while, we both agreed this was the best option."

"Oh, sure. No, it makes total sense."

She didn't say anything further, so Ryder plated his food. After he ate, Fiona remarkably quiet the whole time, he checked his watch. It was only eight. "Are you sure you don't want to watch a movie or something? Might take your mind off things."

Fiona rinsed off his plate and loaded it into the dishwasher. "I'm sure. Let me just grab you some blankets and stuff."

He admired the efficient way she moved as she crossed the condo and retrieved blankets and a pillow from the hall closet and turned the couch into a suitable guest bed. "Sorry, it's not much. Gabbi's been staying in my guest room…"

"It's great. I've slept on worse."

"Sure. I'll see you in the morning, okay?"

"Sounds good. Sweet dreams, Fiona." He nearly whispered that last part, but Fiona's steps faltered just enough to let him know she'd heard him.

He was an idiot.

After shutting off the lights, he pulled off his button-down shirt. Tomorrow he'd need to run to the condo downstairs, but he didn't want to leave Fiona alone, even for a minute. And she was so exhausted, he hated to ask her to come with him tonight. Jeans and his T-shirt would have to do.

He punched some life into the flat pillow and flipped the television to reruns of a sitcom he'd seen a hundred times, turning the volume down low.

The next thing he knew, his eyes flew open and his body tensed. He'd been asleep, but what had woken him up? His eyes strained in the dark, searching for movement in the murky shadows of the unfamiliar apartment. Sliding his hand under the pillow, he laid his finger on the outside of the trigger, waiting for whatever had woken him to make itself known.

His question was quickly answered by another sound. The ding of the elevator in the hallway. He must have heard the door of the condo closing.

Fiona.

He grabbed his gun and ran straight to her

bedroom, only to find it empty. He shoved his feet into his shoes and grabbed his coat as he bolted out the door. He jammed the elevator button repeatedly, then tossed on the jacket and tucked his gun into the pocket. Running down ninety flights of stairs certainly wouldn't be any faster.

Then, he pulled up his phone. He opened the app that allowed him to track Fiona's phone. She was still in the building. As he rode the elevator down, he saw the small blue dot move west.

Did someone have her? Or was she sneaking out on her own? The idea that someone could have snuck in while he dozed on the couch seemed impossible. But she'd obviously made it out the door without being detected.

Was this why she'd been so cagey after Gabbi was hurt? There was something she wasn't telling him. And this late-night escape had something to do with it. Where did she think she was going?

He jogged through the lobby and onto the street. Street lights and neon signs assaulted him, and the angry red of brake lights reflected on the slippery streets as traffic lined up at the signal.

Searching the sidewalks, scanning for any sight of her. A man bumped into him. "Watch it, man."

There were still quite a few people out, despite the

chilly January air. The city that never sleeps was living up to its name. No sign of her. He checked his phone again. A block away, moving fast. She must be in a car.

He hailed a cab as fast as he could, grateful when one stopped after just a minute. How was it in the movies that a person was always able to get a cab moments after they stuck their hand in the air?

When the driver asked where to, Ryder looked at the map, locking on to the nearest landmark beyond the current path of the blue dot.

"Times Square."

"You got it."

When they arrived at the busy intersection, he tossed some cash in the front seat and climbed out, scanning the area. Tourists filled the sidewalks, snapping selfies and taking videos of the iconic New York landmark.

She could be anywhere. There were a dozen hotels, countless restaurants and about ten thousand people within these city blocks. A needle in a haystack.

"Come on, Fiona. Where are you?"

He looked at the tracker, zooming in for more context. He had to be close.

A flash of long, dark hair and a familiar red coat

caught his eye down the sidewalk. He ran up and grabbed her shoulder. But the face that glared back at him wasn't Fiona's.

"Sorry, I thought you were…" he trailed off as he saw her. She was sitting on the Red Stairs at the north end of Times Square. She looked around nervously. He started running toward her, simultaneously surveying the area. This was a tactical nightmare.

Fiona was isolated and exposed from about a million directions. He ran up the steps, dodging couples huddled together on the steps. Why were there so many people here?

He checked his watch. 11:57 p.m.

"Fiona!" he called when he was close enough.

She looked up at him in surprise and fear. "You can't be here! They'll see you!"

"See me? Fiona, they'll kill you! What were you thinking?"

She hung her head. "They just wanted money. I'm here to give it to them. Then this whole thing can just go away. They should have been here by now."

"Please, Fiona." He looked around helplessly. The stalker could be anywhere. "Come with me."

She shook her head. "I don't think they're coming. They should have been here by now." She looked so worried.

He swallowed his frustration. He couldn't exactly carry her forcibly through the street. If they were going to die, he might as well sit with her.

He sat on the steps. He was close enough to see the tear tracks on her cheeks, and he brushed one away with his fingers.

"Tell me what happened."

"An email. Said to meet them here with fifty thousand dollars."

His eyebrows shot up. "You have fifty grand with you right now? Are you crazy?"

"I just want it all to go away!"

"Oh, honey. It's not going to be that easy."

"Why didn't they come?"

"I don't know. But I'm glad they didn't." The flickering lights from all the billboards went dark and cheers rose from the crowd. He tensed. "What's going on?"

"It's the Midnight Moment. It's an art thing. Happens every night."

He relaxed at her words. He vaguely remembered it from living here. That explained the crowd scattered on the steps. The screens around them synchronized with a swirling array of abstract color. For three minutes, the adrenaline faded and he simply watched. Fiona leaned into him. When the art show faded and the screens resumed their colorful advertising, she whispered, "I'm sorry."

He sighed. "I'm just glad nothing–"

His words were cut off by the sound of gunfire. It was difficult to tell where it was coming from. Screams erupted around them, and Ryder quickly covered Fiona with his body as he ushered her toward the edge of the steps. He saw the impact of bullets on the steps behind them. "Move!"

People scattered, but the shots stopped. Ryder peeked over the ledge they hid behind and scanned the area. Others were doing the same from wherever they had taken shelter. He couldn't see a shooter at all. Had it been a sniper?

"Come on." He grabbed Fiona's arm and led them down the street, careful to keep her shielded and staying close to buildings or cars. He didn't breathe until they ducked into the closest subway station. Out of any sightlines.

It didn't make sense that no one had shown up to take the money. Unless he was right and they weren't after money. Surely, they had opportunities to hurt Fiona before tonight. So why now? And what else would they have accomplished by doing this?

Two days later at work, he got his answer.

Fiona's temporary assistant, Ashley, came into the

office. She held out a handful of papers hesitantly. She had none of the confidence and spunk of Gabbi, that was for sure.

"Umm, Ms. Raven. I think you're going to want to see these."

Fiona frowned. "What is it?" She came around the desk and grabbed the papers, then a string of unfamiliar Italian came from her mouth.

He stood to take a look. Fiona practically threw the stack of papers at him and he grabbed it. "Tabloids? Really, Ashley?"

Then he looked…and saw just why Fiona was so upset.

CHAPTER
THIRTEEN

SHE WATCHED as Ryder flipped through the papers, reading the now-familiar headlines. *Culinary Queen and Her Secret Lover.* The bold heading was displayed above images of them on the steps, looking awfully intimate. There were more photos of them walking into her building with takeout.

He shuffled to the next paper. *Rustic Raven Star's Sordid Affair* followed by *Foodie Fiona Fights with Secret Fiancé.*

That was a fun twist. Ryder frowned. "Fiancé?"

That one had a photo of the two of them in the heated discussion. She knew it was him scolding her for sneaking out and trying to convince her to come with him. But it looked like any lover's quarrel.

"Good thing I vetoed the idea of carrying you out

over my shoulder. That would've made a good cover shot."

Fiona couldn't help the laugh that escaped at his comment. "You wouldn't have."

"Oh, I seriously considered it. For good reason, apparently."

One last paper prominently displayed the headline: *Cooking CEO Heartbroken by Bad Boy Bodyguard.*

"At least they got the bodyguard part right," she said. It was above a photo of her sitting alone on the steps. Even she was surprised at how desperately sad she appeared.

"Whoa. That's some major fiction they are peddling." He tossed the papers on her desk. "There's a shooting in Times Square and *this* is what they choose to print? What a joke."

Fiona buried her head in her hands. "This is humiliating, Ryder!" Fiona felt like an idiot. She knew she'd been tricked, but she'd honestly just wanted so badly for paying them off to be the solution. She would give the guy some money and he could disappear back into whatever hole he crawled out of.

Instead, they'd tried to kill her. And now? If they couldn't get her with a bullet, they seemed intent on humiliating her instead. She wasn't sure what was worse.

Maybe that was a bit dramatic. But she would finish her pity party in a minute. Then she'd have to call WBC back and beg them not to take away her Valentine's Day special. She needed the exposure the episode would give her. The Valentine's Day show was the most popular *Date Night America* episode, airing the Sunday before the holiday.

"Nah." He shrugged. "Now, losing my bathing suit jumping off the diving board at Camp Huckabay in 8th grade? That was humiliating. This is…gossip. Lies. Nobody reads these, Fi."

Ashley came back in. "I've got calls from Entertainment Tonight and all the major networks. Marvin from WBC wants you to call him, also."

Fiona breathed deeply. So much for that theory. "This is a nightmare. It might not be a big deal for you, because who cares if the NYPD washout has a fight with his pretend girlfriend?" She saw Ryder flinch and it made her falter. Still, she continued. "But my entire brand is built on being wholesome *and* professional. A role model. Not someone who sneaks around with her bodyguard."

"But you haven't."

He had a point. Maybe they'd shared a few

moments here and there. But no matter how she wished it could be different, they would never be together. But even these rumors that they were dating could be catastrophic to her image.

"One thing you learn in the entertainment business: the truth doesn't matter–only the perception."

————

That night after dinner, Ryder's phone rang and he saw an unfamiliar number.

"Ryder McClain." He stood from the sofa and began pacing, like he usually did when he talked on the phone.

"Hey, Mac, it's Cheno. I've got that footage. Like I said before, the plates on the van came back stolen. But I'll send you a link to the videos if you want them. It's a little gruesome."

"Got it. Shoot me the link and I'll take a look." And he'd be sure not to let Fiona see. The last thing she needed was to see a video of her best friend getting run down.

Careful to keep one eye on Fiona across the room, he watched the video. The driver jumped the curb and headed straight for Gabbi. It was definitely no accident. His anger rose sharply as he saw her unsuccessfully try to dodge the speeding van.

He quickly forwarded the link to Joey. If anyone could get something off the video, it was her.

She called him back mere minutes later.

"What do you have for me, Joey?"

"I'm not sure. I've got stolen plates on the van, but they were stolen four months ago. And get this, the plates are registered to a Prius."

"So, they stole the plates, not the van." Apparently, these guys were covering their tracks.

"Exactly. The Prius is registered in Hoboken."

He didn't care about the Prius. "What about the van?"

"The logo on the side of the van was painted over, but I was able to make out the shape. As far as I can tell, it is the logo of a catering company from Long Island. They went out of business last year."

He smiled. She was the best for a reason. "I don't suppose there's a record of who purchased their assets?"

"As a matter of fact, I was able to get the VIN from the registration records of the company. That van is now registered to—get this—a subsidiary of Citadel Security."

Ryder bit back a curse. He'd dealt with Citadel in

his previous life. They were hired mercenaries, involved in everything from drugs to guns to government black ops. Shane Lowell, the owner, was a master at playing both sides of a conflict and making sure he was ultimately the one who came out ahead.

"Give me everything you've got."

Citadel was just the hired muscle. He needed to figure out who hired them, though.

"Sending it to you now. Be careful, Mac."

The next morning, he connected with Daniels. After arranging for someone from the security team to stand in his place, he waited in Fiona's office for them to show up.

When a skinny, middle-aged man in a white shirt and blue baseball cap showed up outside the glass wall, Ryder raised his eyebrows. Not exactly intimidating people with the muscle on the Raven Foods security team.

Fiona frowned at the knock on the door and then looked at him. "What's going on? Why is Ray here?"

"I've got a lead and I need to go check it out. Ray is going to take my place for a bit."

She stood up and held up a finger to let Ray know they needed a minute. "What's the lead?" She crossed the room toward him, rubbing the back of her arms as she wrapped them around herself.

"I don't even know if it is anything yet." He didn't want to get her hopes up. There was a good chance this was a dead end. With all of Joey's powers, it was a longshot.

Fiona was next to him now and she looked up. "Please tell me?"

Her dark-brown eyes were vulnerable and soft and he felt himself caving. How was he powerless against this woman? He groaned.

"It's just a lead right now."

"Take me with you."

"Yeah, right."

"I'm serious. This is my business being targeted. My friends. My life."

He tucked a strand of hair behind her ear. "You are incredibly smart and brave. And there is no way on God's green earth that I am taking you to look into someone who may or may not own the van that ran down your friend and tried to kill her. For one, because Flint would never forgive me if anything happened to you, and two, because I would never forgive myself."

She must have been mollified by that explanation because she sucked in a breath and nodded. "Fine. But be careful."

"Careful, princess. I might start thinking you care."

She looked up into his eyes. "I do care, Ryder."

For a moment, Ray and the rest of the plush office ceased to exist. Ryder stared into her eyes—dark brown and flecked with gold—as the worry and emotion he saw there eased an ache he didn't realize he carried.

Before he'd even had time to contemplate the action, his face lowered and his lips met hers. Her gasp of surprise was silenced as he finally gave in to the longing he'd carried since he first met his best friend's little sister when she was barely eighteen and he was an optimistic college student about to join the police academy.

He would do anything for Flint, but he wasn't sure he would be able to leave Fiona alone, especially after this. Her lips were soft and sweet beneath his, and he savored the feel of them as she hummed her approval. When the kiss broke, Fiona touched her delicate fingertips to her lips as she stared at a point near his shoulder.

She stammered. "I-uh…you…"

He reached a hand up and trailed his fingers down her cheek. "I should go." There was nothing more that he wanted than to stay and spend the day exploring

Fiona's lips. But he couldn't ignore all the reasons he couldn't do that.

Her brother. His friend. A lead in the case. Her reputation. His reputation.

Her eyes closed and she leaned her cheek into his touch before nodding and stepping back. "Yeah. You probably should."

He took a step toward the door and then stopped when she called his name. He turned to find her behind her desk, shoulders back and a familiar stubborn look on her face.

"We'll talk more about this later."

He couldn't help the crooked smile that spread across his face. She was incredible. And fearless. The flirty comment sprang to his lips before he thought better of it. "You bet your tiara we will."

CHAPTER FOURTEEN

FIONA WATCHED Ryder disappear out the office door and averted her eyes when Ray stepped in. How much had the security guard seen?

As much as she'd relished the kiss and the tender expression on Ryder's face when he said goodbye, the young officer in a gray Raven Foods's uniform was an unwelcome reminder that she still stood to lose everything. And with the tabloids already screaming about her and Ryder, it was only a matter of time before any actual relationship with him was under a microscope.

It was the unfortunate reality that came with her fame. She might not be Angelina Jolie, but Fiona found herself featured in Hollywood chatter more often than she would like. And if things went the way she wanted, with her on-camera work expanding to not only include her cable cooking show but a daytime network spot? She'd be even more of a target for rumors and speculation.

Was it all worth it?

She thought again of Ryder. He definitely wasn't the Upper East Side clean-cut investment banker the magazines usually tried to pair her with. One would think sitting together at a single fundraiser meant she was nearly engaged to a person.

No, Ryder was an entirely different kind of man. Rough around the edges, strong, and steadfast. With his dark eyes, strong jaw, and mysterious past, Ryder was every woman's bad boy fantasy come to life. Including hers.

But even if her dreams about Ryder had started when she was barely a woman and hardly knew him, she knew him now. She knew that beneath the rugged exterior and snarky comments was a heart of gold, loyal to a fault.

And the way he looked at her…

The phone on her desk rang, snapping her out of her daydreams. Time to get back to work. Gabbi would be discharged from the hospital tomorrow, coming back to Fiona's house. The week ahead would be exhausting, with the official practice run for her

Date Night America special–which thankfully the network hadn't canceled–her own secret practice run, and the event itself.

Plus, the birthday party for a friend she couldn't get out of going to. She hadn't actually mentioned that one to Ryder. No doubt he was going to be thrilled. She said a quick prayer that he was doing okay on his errand this morning. Errand? Mission? Recon? What did you call it when you were trying to find clues to someone trying to kill the person you were protecting?

––––––

Ryder tucked away all his feelings about the kiss in Fiona's office as he parked the black SUV he'd borrowed from the Raven Foods fleet. He looked at the building with a sinking feeling. The address Joey had given him in Brooklyn led him to a warehouse as generic as he'd ever seen.

The problem was he had seen it before. The raid at this address twelve years prior had broken up the largest human trafficking operation in New York City history.

His vehicle was out of place amidst the trucks that were traversing the wide roads. Nothing looked suspicious about the building itself. An old painted sign proclaimed it as Pullman Brother's Shipping, and all the garage bays were closed.

Ryder climbed out and grabbed his weapon, just in case. He slipped on his Bluetooth headset and called Joey.

"I've got a problem, Joey. I've been here before."

"What do you mean?"

"It's a long story. But find me everything you've got on this building."

He heard Joey warning him to wait, but he disconnected the call. Last time he was here, he had a different vantage point. And this was his chance to look around.

He peered through the windows, remembering how twelve years ago, he'd looked through the same windows through the scope of a sniper rifle. He was wishing he had the infrared drone images, too. It looked abandoned, but unless he went inside, there was no way to be sure.

He considered calling Flint right then, but from the various updates he was getting from the rest of the team, their mission hadn't been going well, and Flint was probably putting out fires. Literal or metaphorical were equal possibilities.

Instead, Ryder tugged on the ball cap he wore to

make sure his face was obscured and made his way around the building.

He desperately wished he'd been on the infiltration team when SWAT had raided the warehouse. His vantage point from the roof across the street had been perfect at the time, but now he was wishing he'd been inside.

As far as he could tell, there was no activity inside the warehouse. The windows on the first floor were few and far between. Last time he was here, he'd been able to watch from his sniper position through the windows higher on the building.

When he came to the side door, held his gun at the ready and then wiggled the door handle. As he'd expected, it was locked. Should he break in?

His internal dilemma was interrupted by the sound of ringing in his ear.

He answered with a touch to the earbud. "Go for Mac."

Joey's voice came over the line. "Where are you?"

"I'm in Barbados. Where do you think I am?" He tucked himself against the brick while he talked.

"Don't be a smart aleck. Do you want the info or not?"

"You know I do."

"The Citadel subsidiary that owns the van and the

building? Turns out it is half-owned by Trip Harrington."

He tried to place the name but came up blank. "Is that supposed to mean something to me?"

"Only if you routinely watch the investment news channel. Charles Harrington the Third, AKA Trip, is on the Board of Directors for half a dozen Fortune 500 companies. Sending you his photo."

Ryder rolled his eyes. He hated this guy already. The text beeped on his phone and he looked at the photo. Trip was mid-forties, perfect hair, and a plastic smile. The guy looked like a Ken doll.

He tucked his phone away and looked back at the door to the building. "What do they want with an old warehouse?"

"Not sure. They only bought it a few months ago."

Hmm. Could it be coincidence that they'd raided this same warehouse twelve years ago?

"I don't like it. Citadel isn't a player I want anywhere near Fiona. And I don't know enough about Trip Harrington to make a call."

"I'm just telling you what I found. The guy donates millions to charity. There is a hospital wing named after him. It honestly looks like the address is a coincidence. Except for one thing…" She took a deep breath. "There's a few articles that report Fiona and Trip dating."

He stilled. "What?"

"I can't tell how serious it was, but the articles span a few months. There are photos of the two of them. Maybe this is a lover's quarrel gone south?"

"Maybe. Thanks, Joey."

He pressed the button on his earbud to end the call. Then, with the unwelcome image of Fiona cozied up to Mr. Incredible in his mind, he kicked open the door.

––––––––

Fiona glared at Ray's silhouette outside her door. He was far easier to boss around than Ryder and hadn't even put up a fight when she insisted he sit outside.

Her phone rang and Fiona answered it with a smile. "Gabbi!"

"I think I can bribe the nurse if you front me the money."

Fiona laughed. Clearly, after two days in the hospital, Gabbi was itching to break out.

"No way. Come on, just a couple more days, right?"

"At least three. Or that's what I think they said.

I don't know, the pain meds are pretty strong," Gabbi replied with a sigh. "Do I get to see you today?"

Fiona had spent most of the afternoon there yesterday, avoiding the calls to her office about her torrid affair. After Gabbi had lectured her on her foolish choice to meet the blackmailer, they'd talked about everything but the ongoing threats.

"I'm not sure. Ryder had to leave and so I'm basically stuck here until he gets back."

There must have been something in her voice, because Gabbi's response was far too animated.

"Okay, spill it. What happened?"

Fiona blushed, remembering the tender moment before he left. "It's nothing. Or…it's something. I don't know yet."

"Yesss!" Gabbi hissed the word in celebration. "Give me every detail. Seriously, I need some entertainment. They don't even have Netflix in here."

Fiona opened her mouth to share what had happened but was interrupted by a knock on the door. "Just a second, Gab." She looked expectantly at Ashley. "What's up?"

"Sorry to interrupt. I have those documents from PrimoPak foods you wanted. Antonio from Finance is waiting in the conference room to go over them with you. There was nothing on your schedule, so I told him now was good."

She smiled and pushed down the irritation. The woman was being ambitious and helpful, despite it only being her second day on the job. "Thanks, Ashley. I'll be right in."

Gabbi sighed in her ear. "Duty calls?"

"Sorry, hon. We'll talk later?"

"Fine. But you owe me juicy details, you hear? Juicy details!"

Fiona chuckled as she hung up the call. She missed Gabbi's presence at the office. And while she didn't mind Ryder sleeping on her couch, Gabbi's personal things still filled the bathroom. Which made her remember why Gabbi wasn't there but her things were.

Everything came back to this mysterious threat. She said a prayer that Ryder was onto something that could put an end to it. Then she grabbed the file Ashley left on her desk and walked out of her office. "Let's go, Ray," she said as she passed him, not waiting for him to catch up as she strode down the hallway.

Maybe turning an under-utilized food processing plant into a boutique supplier of jarred pasta sauces would lift her spirits.

———————

As Ryder drove back to the city, he ran over the connections in his head. The van that ran over Gabbi likely traced back to Citadel and Trip Harrington. Trip and Fiona may have dated. Citadel owned the building. Inside, he hadn't found anything incriminating. It looked mostly the same as he remembered over a decade ago.

There was a lot that didn't add up. There had to be something here, though. The best guess he had right now was Trip taking a broken heart to violent levels. Fiona had never even mentioned the guy, though. He'd definitely have to ask her about Trip; he had someone else in mind who might be able to give some insight.

When the call connected, a deep male voice greeted him. "Cole Kensington."

Ryder paused. He hadn't expected to reach him directly. Didn't billionaires have people answer the phone for them?

"Uh, hey, Mr. Kensington. This is Ryder McClain from Black Tower. I'm staying at your condo?"

"Of course. I hope it's working out for you. Did you call about the condo?"

"No, no. The place is great. It's way more than I

need, honestly. I was actually calling about something else. You know Fiona Raven, right?"

"Of course. Even if she weren't my neighbor, everyone knows Fiona. I was sorry to hear she was having security troubles."

Ryder knew the purpose of his call, but he couldn't help but wonder just how neighborly Cole and Fiona had been. The two of them would be well-suited… Just the kind of successful businessman Fiona would end up with.

"Have you and Fiona ever…dated?"

Cole's chuckle made some of the tension release from Ryder's shoulder. "No, unfortunately not. Not for lack of trying on my part, though. The woman is as driven as I've ever seen. We've talked a few times, but there isn't any spark, you know? She's just a bit closed off."

No spark with Fiona? No, Ryder couldn't relate to that. He searched for the right words. "Okay, that's fine. I just had to ask. I did have one other question."

"Sure, whatever you need." He was beginning to like this guy more and more.

"What can you tell me about Trip Harrington?"

A low whistle came through the speaker. "Trip? I know the rumors said he and Fiona were together a while back, but I'd be shocked if it were true. Trip's public persona of the benevolent billionaire doesn't exactly hold up with anyone who has spent more than an hour with the man."

That was interesting, but hardly surprising. "What do you mean?"

"I'll be frank. He's a narcissistic cutthroat who will do anything to win. I've managed to mostly avoid him, but it's almost impossible in our circles. From what I know of Fiona, she's truly a good person. She wouldn't be able to stand Trip for one date, let alone several. She's sweet, but Trip is toxic. She's smarter than that."

Ryder breathed a sigh of relief. "That's good to hear. Do you think Trip would have taken a rejection personally?"

Cole chuckled. "Not a chance. He thinks far too highly of himself. If Fiona rejected him, it wouldn't even faze him. He'd just move on to the next."

"Thanks, Cole. I appreciate the info."

"No problem, I hope it helps. Flint is a good friend, and I would hate to see something happen to Fiona. Call me anytime if you need anything else."

Ryder disconnected the call and mulled over Cole's words. Any ill thoughts he had about the rich bachelor living below Fiona were suddenly much friendlier. Cole seemed like a good guy. But what he said about Trip Harrington was concerning.

Ryder knew men like Trip. They thought they were untouchable. But if Trip Harrington was targeting Fiona, then he was going to find out just what Ryder was capable of.

CHAPTER FIFTEEN

WHEN RYDER finally walked back through the door of Fiona's office, she scowled at him. She looked at her watch. "I didn't know you were going to be gone all day."

"Why wasn't he in here with you?" Ryder gestured at Ray, who was leaving. "He was supposed to stay with you."

"I kicked him out. This is my office. Some things are confidential."

He shook his head in frustration. "Why don't you ever listen?"

Fiona shrugged. "What did you find out?"

"I'm not sure. Let's grab dinner and I'll catch you up." He stood at the door and held it for her.

"Sounds good. I have some things to run through

with you too. The Valentine's special is only one week away, and my calendar is jam-packed."

Of course it was. The woman was moving non-stop. They picked up burgers, and even though Fiona made it clear she would rather sit and eat at the restaurant, Ryder firmly insisted on calling in the order to go.

After he'd cleared the apartment, they went to the kitchen and pulled out the food.

Through bites of burger, Ryder asked the question he'd been dreading. "Fiona, can you think of anyone who would want to hurt you? An ex-boyfriend perhaps?"

Confusion was evident on her face and Fiona shook her head. "It's not like I've really dated anyone. But no. I really can't think of anyone."

He set down his food. "Trip Harrington?"

There was no faking the surprise on her face. "What? Trip? There's no way. There was an awful season a few years ago where I seemed to be seated next to him at every event I attended. He's the most obnoxious man in the city."

Well, at least Ryder didn't have to worry about her harboring feelings for the wealthy banker. "Is there any chance *he* thought there was more to it?"

Fiona shook her head. "I doubt it. He might be

obnoxious, but he's not stupid. I was pretty clear I wasn't interested." She paused. "You can't possibly think he has something to do with this?"

Ryder shrugged. "I don't know. It could be nothing, but the van that ran us down is owned by Trip and another company that is known for being hired guns. Could just be coincidence that whoever is after you hired Citadel."

Fiona bit her lip. "It has to be a coincidence. Trip is one of the most influential men in the city. He wouldn't hurt anyone, would he?"

With few exceptions, Ryder believed people clawed their way to the top of the food chain, with little regard to who they hurt on the climb. Trip was undoubtedly no different. The jury was still out on Cole.

———

Ryder tipped a head toward the bedrooms. "Gabbi comes home tomorrow. Andi is going to come stay with her–and you."

Fiona raised her eyebrows. She knew Andi from Flint's stories. The woman had served in the military for twenty years before retiring and starting the security firm with Flint and Ryder's brother, Ross.

She would really come stay with them? "Why?"

Ryder set down his food. "We need another set of hands. The rest of the team is on a mission for another week or so. Andi is going to teach you some self-defense while she's here, and she can stay the night so there is no more fuel for those rumors about us."

Fiona was grateful for the food in her mouth, since it gave her time to think of a response. Those rumors about her and Ryder were inconvenient. But she did feel safer with him close by. Of course, Andi could protect her just as well. So why did the thought that tonight was Ryder's last night sleeping on her couch have her feeling disappointed?

"That seems like a good solution. I've heard a lot about her. It will be good to have a chance to get to know her better."

Ryder smiled. "She's awesome. Andi is the only person I've seen go toe-to-toe with Ross and come out ahead."

"You don't talk about your brother much," she commented, trying to sound casual.

"Yeah, well… Our relationship is complicated. He's the successful big brother. I'm the black sheep." He shrugged. "I love him. But in some ways it was easier when I didn't have to see him every day."

Fiona smiled. "I get that. Flint is great. But his

success is intimidating. Even knowing he walked away from it all."

"His success intimidates you? You're just as successful as he is."

It was her turn to shrug. "Hardly. But his definition of success has changed, hasn't it?"

Ryder nodded. "Yeah, it really has. I watched Flint go from student body president and computer nerd to crazy start-up dreamer turned tech mogul. Then when your mom died, I lived with him as he left Raven Tech behind and embraced a part of him I'd never seen before. When Jessica needed him, he proved himself a warrior. And now, he's going to be a father."

Fiona watched his expression carefully as Ryder expounded on the journey her brother had taken. "And what about you? Surely, he's seen you go through changes as well?"

Ryder clicked his tongue. "You'd think so. But no. I'm pretty much the same aimless guy I've always been." Ryder crumpled up the wrapper of his burger and shoved it in the bag as he stood.

She cleared her throat and cleared the table, turning her back to Ryder in the kitchen. "Aimless? Don't you have any dreams?"

"Not really."

She jumped at the closeness of his voice. She turned to find Ryder directly behind her, nearly trapping her against the kitchen table.

He continued, "It's probably better that way. When I want something too much, it tends to slip through my fingers." His eyes seared a path from her head to her toes. Fiona felt the gaze as if it were a physical caress.

Emboldened, she tipped her head up to meet his eyes in a challenge. "I think you're just afraid to admit what you want. Easier to maintain your tough-guy persona if you keep everyone at a distance."

"Maybe you're right. It's an interesting theory."

His thighs brushed hers and her mind went blank. What theory?

"There is something I want," he admitted.

Yes! He wanted her. She could feel it in her bones. Inside, she was celebrating, but she nodded solemnly. "That's good. See? Not aimless."

His mouth lifted in a crooked grin. "What should I do about it, then?"

She sucked in a breath. "Well, I think…*pursuing* the things you want is an admirable quality. As long as those things aren't selfish or illegal."

He chuckled. "Oh, the thing I want to do would be very selfish."

Fiona tipped her head to one side. "I doubt that."

He leaned in, his mouth stopping near her ear. She could feel his breath on her neck and every nerve ending in her body went on hyper alert. "Flint would say otherwise," he whispered.

As his words registered, he stepped back. The warmth and awareness from his closeness was gone and her entire body nearly sagged with the sudden loss of tension. She'd been wound tight as a spring waiting for him to admit his feelings, maybe even kiss her and then…nothing.

———

Ryder stood, watching with interest as Andi gave Fiona a self-defense basics lesson. The workshops seemed hokey, until you realized the techniques could literally be the difference in someone living and dying. And when that someone was Fiona? Well, he didn't find it so amusing.

"Mac, get over here and stand in." Andi's command left no room for argument—no doubt a skill she'd acquired during her twenty years in the Army.

His sister-in-law moved him so he was face-to-face with Fiona. She looked cute in her workout clothes and her blonde hair pulled back in one of those fluffy ponytail holders. She stuck her tongue out at him with a funny face.

Andi stood to the side. "I want you to put your hands around her throat."

His eyes widened and he turned to Andi. "What? No way!"

"This is important. You're the attacker. She'll learn better from you, since you're more likely the size of someone."

Everything felt completely wrong about the movement, but he slowly placed his open hands around her neck. His thumbs rested lightly on the smooth skin and he could feel her pulse racing.

He'd held men around the neck before. He'd even applied pressure until they gasped for air. His stomach heaved at the thought of someone holding Fiona in this position.

Everything within him screamed at even pretending to hurt her, when in his very core he only longed to protect her. He looked in her eyes, a hint of amusement and a firm resolve.

This was the best way to protect her. Which meant he would ignore the ugly feeling that came from holding her so vulnerably.

Andi walked Fiona through the instinctual

response of trying to grab Ryder's arms to remove them. He held tight as she tugged, because that's what a real attacker would do.

Then Andi showed her the more effective technique of slipping out of his grasp. "Good! See how if you can break his grip at his thumbs, you're able to get away?"

He watched with admiration as Fiona practiced the move over and over again.

Until it was perfect.

They repeated the process with more positions. It got easier to play the part and be just a training partner. With one arm, he pinned her against the wall and let her work through the pivot and arm strike combo that would let her escape.

When the training session was over, they ordered dinner and stood around the kitchen counter.

He raised his pizza in a salute. "Thanks again for coming, Andi."

Fiona grunted through a full mouth, swallowing quickly. "Oh, yes. Thank you."

"No problem. I'm happy to help. I wish I could stay longer, though."

"I'm just glad you'll be around for this birthday party." He raised an eyebrow at Fiona. "Are you sure we can't send a card instead?" Ryder was dreading an evening at the famous New York nightclub.

Fiona shook her head. "Sorry. Trust me, I'd rather stay home with you too."

Ryder stuffed the last bit of his pizza in his mouth and tried not to analyze what Fiona meant when she said she wanted to "stay home with you." Because since Gabbi was hurt, they'd spent every evening together. She cooked or they got takeout, and they turned on the TV while she worked on her laptop. It was…very domestic. And he wasn't complaining at all.

———

Fiona finished curling her hair and stepped forward so Andi could sneak behind her to the other side of the vanity. Andi was a bit older than herself, but Fiona thought she was beautiful. Her confidence was unmatched. Not as boisterous as Gabbi, but understated. Firm.

She met Andi's eyes in the mirror. "You look lovely."

Andi made a face. "I don't remember the last time I was in a nightclub. Ryder is going to owe me for this one."

Fiona's smile froze in place. "Oh. You—you don't have to come with us."

Andi's eyes widened. "Oh, honey. That's not what I meant. I just mean I'll give Ryder a hard time. He's my brother-in-law, and in my family, that means you get your chain yanked a bit."

Her hand came to rest on Fiona's shoulder. "I'm glad I'm here to help, Fiona."

Fiona blew out a shaky breath. "Me too. I'm sure you'd rather be home with your husband."

Andi chuckled as she grabbed for her makeup bag. "Probably, but Ross is out in Los Angeles anyway. I'd be curled up with a book if I weren't here."

"That sounds nice," Fiona said. After a moment, she turned back to Andi. "Do you mind if I ask you a question?"

"Shoot."

"When you and Ross met…how did you know he was…it?"

Andi smiled. "Well, I'm not sure Ross and I are a good template, since we pretty much argued for the first four months we knew each other. But once I realized how serious our feelings were… It became impossible to imagine a future without each other."

"And Ross gave up his career for you?" Fiona

couldn't imagine asking Ryder to stop working at Black Tower. But Ross and Andi had both given up a lot to be together. Was she willing to do that for Ryder?

Andi laughed. "Oh, no. Not exactly. Turns out, God had something bigger planned that would involve both of us. Black Tower Security wasn't just Ross's dream. It was a way for both of us to work together doing something we were passionate about."

Fiona smiled at that. She admired the way Andi spoke of God's plan for her life. "What exactly do you do at BTS?"

Andi shrugged. "I'm in charge of the pro-bono operations. Flint and Ross bring in the paying clients. I volunteer teaching self-defense classes around the area…and when I come across someone who needs a little extra help, I bring it in-house."

Fiona's eyes widened. "Oh, wow. I had no idea. I knew Flint mentioned helping people like Jessica, but I didn't know how it worked.

Andi smiled. "We don't exactly publicize that part. But we've helped some people in a lot of trouble. Ryder especially. He seems to gravitate toward the pro-bono missions."

"Oh?" She considered that new piece of information, filed it away with the rest of the ever-growing positive traits of Ryder McClain.

Andi's green eyes met hers with a kind expression. "He's one of the good ones, Fiona. He just doesn't think so yet. Just…don't break his heart, okay?"

Fiona swallowed and nodded, sliding the mascara back in her makeup bag. That was the last thing she wanted to do.

CHAPTER
SIXTEEN

FIONA WEAVED through the guests of the party, being held at an exclusive nightclub in Manhattan. It wasn't her scene, but rumors would fly if she didn't attend the shindig hosted by the fellow cooking show host, Stacy Shipman. They weren't exactly friends, but there was no ill-will either, no matter how hard the tabloids tried to create a rivalry between them.

The music blared and across the club, the dance floor was a throng of bodies that shifted and moved to the beat that united them. She stayed far from the mass of partiers, confidently approaching the VIP section. She pointed to Ryder and Andi, yelling to the bouncer over the music, "They're with me."

The man unclipped the velvet rope and let them

through. She could feel Ryder close behind, knew his eyes were roving, taking in all of the surroundings. Did he feel as out of place here as she did? Or did he frequent loud, sweaty nightclubs when he wasn't working? She found a booth and slid onto the white leather cushions. The booth had been designed to isolate the group sitting, with chairs that rose up and created a small cave.

Ryder sat across from her. "What now?" Despite their distance from the dance floor, she wouldn't have heard him if he hadn't spoken loudly. Though he spoke to her, his eyes were on the outside world.

She shrugged. "Now, we hang out for a bit. Then I give Stacy a hug, say happy birthday, snap a selfie, and we get out of here in time to catch *Saturday Night Live* in our sweatpants."

Andi smiled. "That sounds more like it."

Fiona nodded. "For me too. I appreciate you coming tonight." She spotted Stacy across the VIP section. "I can't afford any hint of trouble ahead of the Valentine's special. And the press is always trying to manufacture a feud between me and Stacy."

Ryder frowned. "Why would they do that?"

"Ratings, I guess. We're both single, young chefs with television shows. They like the idea that we would be competing." She smiled. "Which, we do.

But only in the kitchen. We've done a couple of competition shows for charity. But Stacy's sweet and it never gets ugly. I sent her flowers when she opened her new restaurant. She sent me chocolate when I had the ribbon cutting for Chicago."

She shook her head. "Still, no matter what either of us say, the tabloids seem convinced we can't work in the same sphere without getting catty."

Andi rolled her eyes. "Heaven forbid women just support each other and cheer each other on."

Fiona nodded. "Exactly. So, here we are."

A server dressed in all white came to their table with an iPad in hand. They placed their drink orders, receiving raised eyebrows when Ryder and Andi only ordered soda water with lime.

"Oh my goodness! Is that Fiona Raven?"

The high-pitched squeal from the woman nearly made her wince, but Fiona forced a smile. "Hi, Charity."

"Don't you 'Hi, Charity' me. I saw online that you're engaged? I was just shocked that I hadn't heard anything about it. And I just know you wouldn't start planning a wedding without talking to me!"

Fiona's smile wavered. "Nope, not engaged. Just

another over-ambitious reporter… You know how they are, don't you?"

Charity gasped. "Oh my, yes. Of course. I can't believe they would print such lies. But…" Her glance flicked to Ryder. "Isn't this him? I must say, the photos didn't do him justice." Charity gave him a once-over. "Please tell me the dating rumors are true at least."

"He's my bodyguard, Charity."

Charity waved a hand. "Pssh. You say that like they can't both be true. You know Missy Evans married the man her daddy hired to guard her right? Mr. Evans was downright furious. Nearly refused to pay for the wedding." Charity leaned in and whispered like she was telling a terrible secret. "*We almost ended up with fake flowers in the centerpieces.*"

Fiona glanced at Ryder who was hiding a smile.

"The horror!" Fiona replied sarcastically, but Charity didn't get the joke.

"I know! It would have been an embarrassment. But, Daddy Warbucks came through and everything went off without a hitch. Other than the groom punching out the ex-boyfriend, but the wedding planner can hardly be blamed for that, am I right? It was all very shocking, but I must admit, kind of sexy when he got all possessive like that." Charity eyed Ryder again. "I wonder if it's a bodyguard thing…"

Fiona had never been more grateful for a glass of wine to appear as she was in that moment.

She lifted her glass and toasted. "To the birthday girl."

"If you'll excuse me, Charity, I need to hit the ladies room. Andi, would you come with me?"

"No problem. I'll just stay here and get to know your muscle man over here."

Ryder's expression was one of panic as Fiona and Andi stood up. She took pity on him. "Actually, Mac, maybe now would be a good time for you to make that phone call you mentioned? There's a quiet room for calls near the restrooms."

He stood eagerly, clutching his glass. "Definitely. Very important phone call."

Fiona waved to Charity. "Good to see you, Charity. Enjoy your night."

————

Ryder followed Fiona and Andi toward the restrooms. He sipped his soda water. He was starting to believe the only risk at this party was the threat of superficial socialites.

The restrooms were down a quiet hall, and the loud thrum of music faded until just the pounding bass could be felt through his feet. Fiona stumbled slightly before she and Andi disappeared into the restroom. He took the opportunity to do the same. Inside, an attendant stood near a small table with mints, small bottles of mouthwash, cologne, Q-tips, and earplugs.

After washing his hands, he slipped the mouth-wash and earplugs into his pocket and tipped the man ten bucks. "Thanks, man."

"Have a good evening, sir."

He stepped back into the hallway, but there was no sign of Andi and Fiona. A few minutes later, he heard Fiona's voice. Louder than usual, she was giggling. "Have you *seen* him? That body!"

He chuckled. She'd barely had a drink. Was Fiona tipsy? More importantly…was she talking about him?

Andi came out, supporting Fiona's weight as Fiona stumbled on her heels. Her words slurred as she continued her speech. "I'm just saying… There's no way Santa fits down the chimney. Do they think kids are dumb?"

Fiona looked at him and gasped. "I know you!" She stumbled out of Andi's arms and into his. "You're so strong." Then she grinned. "Hold me?"

He frowned and looked at Andi. "What the heck?"

"I don't know, Mac. She's three sheets to the wind."

"You know as well as I do that she's had one drink. Half a drink!" Her half-empty wine glass was still on the table in the hallway. That could only mean one thing. He held Fiona up with one arm, grabbed the glass and held it up to the light. The pale yellow of the white wine was cloudy. They never would have noticed in the dim blue lights of the nightclub. He'd heard how quickly the date-rape drugs worked, but seeing it in action was something else entirely. It hadn't even been fifteen minutes since they toasted at the table.

A trio of rambunctious women came toward them down the hallway. He turned back to Andi and murmured, "She's been drugged. We've got to get her out of here." He issued orders to Andi without thinking. "Keep her close while we walk. We can't make a scene."

Not only did he need to get Fiona out safely, but he had to make sure she didn't embarrass herself. She clung to his waist as Andi tried to get her to walk. "No offense, Andi. But I'd rather walk with Ryder." Her overly flirtatious tone would have tipped him off if her other behavior hadn't. She ran her hand over his chest and he grabbed her wrist.

"Let's just get out of here. Okay, princess?" He bent his knees to meet her eye-to-eye. "Listen, I need you to try to focus. It's going to be loud and exciting out there. But I just need you to concentrate on my voice."

"Issa sexy voice," she slurred.

Oh boy. He looked at Andi. "You take point. I'll follow with her."

Andi nodded. "Let's move."

CHAPTER
SEVENTEEN

FIONA'S WORLD was a blur of sensations. The music enveloped her on all sides, threatening to carry her away in its warmth. She could hear herself talking, but the words seemed fuzzy. Far away.

There was laughter, punctuated by the rainbow flashes of lights. Dancing and overwhelming heat. Why was it so hot?

Smile for the camera. There were hands around her waist. Ryder's tan leather jacket felt soft under her fingers.

She was relaxed. Content. Someone was whispering in her ear. "Come on, princess. We're almost there."

Almost where? She didn't want to leave. She

wanted to dance more. It was fun here. She had no worries. There was only sound and lights and heat.

Then, she was dizzy. Spinning, stumbling, and falling. Hands appeared under her armpits, catching her. His strong arms held her steady against him. She was safe.

Then, her forehead rested against the blissfully cool glass of a window. A car, perhaps? All the previous happiness was gone with only confusion and sadness left in its place. Something was wrong.

She tried to speak through the fog and heaviness around her, but no words came out. Only whimpering. She stared out the window, seeing but not processing.

———————

He followed Andi, weaving in and out of small groups of people as she made her way toward the door. Fiona was having a great time, trying to drag him to the dance floor and attempting to stop for selfies with anyone who recognized her. Ryder put on the controlling boyfriend act and kept them moving. The incessant thumping of the bass and the dim lights felt like an assault. But every unfamiliar shadowy face was a threat.

"Fiona!" Ryder whirled toward the voice. He

recognized Stacy, but the birthday girl sash and crown would have tipped him off otherwise. "You're not leaving already, are you?"

Fiona looked at him with wide, questioning eyes. Trust.

He forced a smile and spoke over the music. "Sorry, Stacey. I'm not feeling well, and Fiona said she'd go back with me. Why don't you guys take a quick picture before we leave?"

He used Fiona's phone to take one. He could see Fiona's eyes were glassy and unfocused, but anyone else wouldn't even notice. Then Stacy was off, pulled aside by another group of women carrying shot glasses. He gripped Fiona's elbow in his hand and pressed toward the exit.

Ryder was still on edge as the cab took them the fourteen blocks back to her building. If he clenched his jaw any tighter, he might chip a tooth. Thank the Lord they'd managed to get Fiona out of the club and into the cab, but it had been dicey. She'd gone from tipsy to wasted to almost despondent in just a matter of minutes.

Ryder opened the door to the apartment, clearing each room carefully before calling the all clear to Andi.

Fiona was awake and walking. But she wasn't

there. The confident, affectionate, happy version from early in the drugging had disappeared. And what was left was an unnerving shell of a woman.

Andi ushered her in. "Why don't you sit down, Fiona?"

Fiona sat.

He grabbed a bottle of water from the fridge and handed it to her, already open. She took it, wordlessly. She stared straight ahead. A zombie.

"Take a drink," he said.

She obeyed. He looked at his sister-in-law in concern. It was unnerving. He was used to Fiona who questioned him at nearly every turn. "Is she going to be all right?"

He knew about roofies. Obviously. But he'd never witnessed the process. He'd never realized how eerily pliable someone was after the drug was fully in their system. Whoever had done this to her could have convinced Fiona to leap off the roof, and she wouldn't bat an eye.

Andi took a drink of her water. "She should be okay. I keep replaying the evening, though. I can't figure out when her drink was spiked. Unless it was the bartender. I've heard about guys paying off the waitstaff, but it's uncommon."

Ryder clenched his jaw. "I'm going back."

Andi raised her eyebrows. "You think that's really a good idea?"

Fiona tipped lazily to one side, laying her head on the armrest of the couch. Her eyes fluttered shut.

A glance at his watch revealed it barely past 11. "I'm going back. Can you put her to bed and make sure she's okay?"

Andi nodded. "Yeah, I've got her. Be careful, Ryder."

"I will."

Ryder grabbed his phone and made a call. "Cheno. You free tonight? I need a favor."

Fifteen minutes later, Ryder was leaning against the building, hands tucked in his pockets. Women in short dresses shivered while they smoked in the freezing night air. Hopeful club attendees waited in the rope line for their time to enter. Down the block, he saw Cheno climbing out of a cab. The police officer had agreed to meet him at the club, in plain clothes as requested.

He stood up and held out a hand to greet his former NYPD brother. "Thanks, man. Fiona is home, hopefully sleeping the drugs out of her system. But I need to go back in and figure out who is behind this."

His friend nodded. "Sure. Where do we start?"

"I've got three suspects." He counted them out on

his fingers. "Bartender. Waitress. And Charity Evans."

"Divide and conquer?"

Ryder nodded. "Let's start in the VIP area. I'll point you to the waitress and I'll talk to Charity. Then we'll handle the bartender together."

Plan confirmed, they approached the door, bypassing the small crowd of dedicated clubbers waiting.

The giant man at the door was dressed in all black, with an earpiece and a clipboard. "Sorry, guys. We're full."

It was so stereotypical that Ryder wanted to laugh. The man was the size of his friend, Tank, but clearly had none of the muscle hiding within his girth. Behind him, the door opened and a few women staggered out, still yelling to be heard, despite the lack of noise outside the club.

Cheno pulled his badge out of his pocket and held it close to his abdomen, discreetly displaying it to the bouncer. "Lucky for us, it looks like space just opened up."

One glance at the badge and the bulky man stepped aside. "Welcome to Bianca Luxe."

Inside, the white interior of the club was dimly lit with blue and red lighting. The music seemed to press in around him, overwhelming his senses with noise and vibrations. He hated clubs.

He got Cheno's attention and pointed to the VIP lounge.

Ryder was extra appreciative of Cheno coming when they had to use his badge again to get into the exclusive area of the club where the birthday party was being held.

At least the music was slightly less deafening up here. They stood near the edge of the elevated lounge while he searched for the server who'd brought their drinks. Finally, he recognized her and pointed her out to Cheno. "Just find out if she knew. If she did, who paid her?"

Cheno nodded and moved to intercept.

Then he took a deep breath and headed into the fray to find Charity. Other than the waitstaff, Charity was the only person who was anywhere close to Fiona while she had her drink.

He didn't have to search for long. Long fingers came around his shoulders from behind, and an annoying nasally voice spoke close to his ear. "I thought that was you, Mr. Bodyguard. Where's Fiona?"

Ryder felt the urge to shudder. Charity was hanging all over him, and it made him want to retch.

He turned so he could see her. She grinned and started dancing.

"Fiona went home," he said in her ear to be heard over the music.

"Oh, well that's a shame. At least she let you stay and enjoy the party." Charity moved closer and tried to grind against him.

He moved to create space between them, but leaned in to talk to her. "Did you do something to Fiona?"

Charity's look of confusion seemed genuine. "What?"

"Do you know why Fiona is sick?" He didn't want to say it. If his gut was right, telling Charity what had happened would be akin to telling the entire city.

"She's sick? That sucks. Is it contagious? I was sitting right next to her! Oh my word. Am I going to get sick too?"

He sighed. This was going nowhere. He looked in her eyes one more time. "You'll be fine. Unless you hurt Fiona. In which case, you'll have to deal with me."

Charity flinched. She took a breath and yelled in his ear. "I'd never hurt Fiona. She's the sweetest person I know. I almost wish she wasn't so perfect, because maybe we could be better friends. But I'm a hot mess, so she just tolerates me. Like everyone else here." Then she stepped back and shrugged. "I hope she's okay."

Ryder nodded and leaned in again. "She'll be okay. And, Charity, you don't have to be perfect for people to like you. Just be you. Lose the fake flirty socialite persona and just let people in. They'll like you."

Charity's eyes were watery when she stepped back. "Thanks." Then, she waved and headed back toward her table. As she did, Ryder saw a skinny man lower his camera, which had been pointed directly at him–and Charity.

CHAPTER
EIGHTEEN

SON OF A GUN. He rushed toward the photographer, but the man disappeared down the steps. Ryder gripped the railing, searching for any sign of the weasel. But he couldn't spot him in the massive crowd on the main dance floor.

He blew out a heavy breath. That could be annoying later. Turning back to the VIP area, he found Cheno heading toward him.

"The waitress was a bust. She nearly cried when I told her a woman was drugged. Said it had happened to her sister once and that she would never do that to another woman. She was either telling the truth or she deserves a Grammy. She did tell me which bartender makes the VIP drinks, but she swears he wouldn't hurt anyone."

"Then I guess it's time to hit the bar."

The bar of the club was massive, spanning the length of one wall. The white-and-clear bar was lit up in blue and purple lights and the name of the club was emblazoned across the mirror behind it.

Five bartenders manned the bar, and there were people three and four deep across the entire length of it. Getting a drink meant first getting the bartender's attention.

"Which one?" he asked Cheno.

He pointed to a scrawny man with a trimmed goatee. "His name is Marcus."

The man grabbed a bottle of liquor from a shelf below the counter and fixed three identical drinks. He traded a man's credit card for the beverages and efficiently swiped the card and handed the receipt. With his other hand, he reached for a drink ticket that a nearby printer issued and began prepping it. Clearly, this wasn't his first day.

Ryder watched him for a minute, then pulled a hundred-dollar bill out of his wallet. The bartender favored patrons with cash, consistently taking their orders before those with cards. Probably figuring the tips would be better.

He held up the bill and the man turned to him. Ryder leaned in and ordered two drinks. The bartender began fixing the drinks and gave him the total. Thirty bucks for two drinks? Ryder raised his eyebrows. Two short cocktails appeared in front of him and Ryder held out the bill. When the bartender reached for it, Ryder pulled it back slightly. "What time do you get off?"

The bartender narrowed his eyes, but his eyes flicked toward the large bill. "Midnight, why?"

Ryder smiled. "Cool. We'll be back, thanks! Keep the change."

The bartender grinned and gave him a friendly nod.

He handed Cheno the drink. "You want one?"

"From the dude who drugged your friend? Yeah, I'll pass."

Ryder smirked. "Yeah, me too. Come on. Let's go wait for the goatee to get off work."

The back entrance of the club was far less impressive. No red carpet, no rope line, and no shivering girls in short dresses inhaling cigarettes. The alley wasn't dirty, but it was still an alley. Dumpsters, cardboard, and lights just a little too far apart. The entrance was barely marked, but the music could be heard through the door. After Officer Chenoweth politely introduced himself to a few young guys hanging out near the entrance to another building, they had the alley all to themselves.

Ryder leaned against the brick wall and fingered the seam on the inside of his pocket. Cheno waited toward the front of the alley.

When the door opened around 12:15, Marcus came out with a few others.

"Marcus!" Ryder called. "You got a minute?"

Marcus looked at Ryder, then his friends. He took off toward the street. Ryder raced after him, sneakers grinding on the dirty concrete of the alley. He pushed past the other employees who had exited with Marcus.

Fifteen yards ahead, Cheno came out of the shadows and intercepted Marcus, pushing him into the brick wall. He held one hand behind Marcus's back, shoving his chest and head and pressing it into the wall so he couldn't move. Ryder was once again grateful he'd brought along backup.

"Just like old times."

Chenoweth chuckled. When Marcus protested, he pushed him harder into the wall. "We'll tell you when we're ready for you to talk."

Ryder bent close to the wall to look at Marcus's smushed face. "Hey there, Marcus. I have a pretty big problem, you see? Because a friend of mine is at home tonight, blitzed out of her mind from a drink at your club."

Marcus panted, "I don't–"

"From a drink that you made. We already know Trish the waitress would have dumped the drink herself if she knew it was drugged. And that leaves you. So you're going to tell me why. And after I'm done with you, I'll tell my friend from the NYPD here whether to recommend you get jail time or just a little slap on the wrist." He turned to Cheno. "It's been a while. What are we looking at? Assault? Possession?"

Chenoweth nodded. "Definitely possession. Probably accessory to an assault charge. That carries, oh… one to three years in prison, if I remember correctly."

Ryder looked back at Marcus for a moment. "I don't think he'd fare well in prison, what do you think?"

"He wouldn't last a week," Cheno confirmed.

"Sounds like you better start talking."

Marcus's eyes were wide with fear when he nodded.

Cheno released his head but kept the bartender's arm pinned behind his back.

"Tell me."

"They threatened my dog, man!" Marcus was nearly in tears at the admission. "I'm so sorry. I didn't want to hurt your friend! But she's all I have, please. She's a purebred Shih Tzu and–"

Ryder snarled. "You drugged an innocent, vulnerable woman to protect *your dog*?" He stepped closer.

Marcus shrank back. "I'm sorry. I'm sorry. Please, I didn't know!"

He grabbed Marcus by the collar. "You didn't know what? That you were putting a woman at risk of assault or kidnapping and torture? Possibly murder?" His voice rose higher, and Marcus winced in response. "You didn't know that the powder you added to her drink would basically turn a brilliant woman into a mindless zombie for someone to take advantage of?"

Disgust overwhelmed him, and Ryder released Marcus's shirt with a shove. Cheno still had a hold of him and he didn't go far.

"Why didn't they just bribe you? Broke New York bartender and all that?"

Marcus made a face. "Are you kidding, bro? I'm a bartender at one of the busiest, high-end clubs in New York. I make four figures *a night* in tips." He rolled his shoulder. "I wouldn't have done it for money," he added pathetically, "but that was my dog."

Ryder paced a small circle before coming back to face Marcus. "Listen here, you little coward." He jabbed a finger into the tender muscle between the collarbone and shoulder blade. "You better count yourself lucky that nothing worse happened tonight. But I'm going to need everything you know about the people who made you do this."

Marcus nodded, and Ryder gave Cheno the signal to release him. Marcus recounted the man who came to the bar, slipping him the drugs with his credit card and letting him know which drink it would be.

"He used a credit card?" Ryder jumped on the detail. "Do you remember the name?"

Marcus shook his head.

"What about his drink?"

Marcus's eyes lit up. "Actually, yeah. He had an Old Fashioned. I mostly make Jack and Cokes and vodka sodas all night, so it stuck out."

That was something. They could get the records from the night and find the credit card. "Anything else you can tell us? What did he look like?"

Marcus shook his head. "I don't even know if I'd recognize him again. Except…he had a tattoo. On the back of his hand." Marcus pointed to the base of his thumb.

"Okay, that helps."

Ryder nodded to Cheno, who flipped into officer mode.

"You realize what a huge mistake you made tonight, right? I don't care if you have Queen Elizabeth's precious little yappers, a dog doesn't even come close to justifying drugging someone. Tell you what I'm gonna do. I'm gonna keep an eye out, and if I so much as hear a rumor about women getting roofied at this club, I'm going to come back for you personally, got it?"

Marcus nodded bleakly.

"Go on. Get home. Don't tell anyone we talked."

After Marcus jogged out of the alley, Ryder grabbed a chunk of concrete and chucked it at the wall in frustration. "Can you believe that guy? *A dog?*"

"Would you rather it be money?" Chenoweth countered.

Ryder grunted in response. He'd rather it not have been at all. But yeah, he was used to dealing with people motivated by money. That was predictable. The fact that whoever had leveraged Marcus had known that money wouldn't motivate him was another piece of the puzzle. He just needed to figure out where it fit.

CHAPTER
NINETEEN

A LOW RUMBLE vibrated around her. Wait. Within her? Where was she? She moaned. Except for the pitiful sound, it was quiet. Not like the club. Wasn't she at the club? She moaned louder, forcing her eyes open against the crushing weight of the headache. It was barely morning, but she could make out a familiar room around her.

The fluffy warmth of her duvet surrounded her. Home? How had she gotten home?

A deep, quiet voice came from the end of the bed. "How are you doing? Are you with me?"

Fiona pressed a hand to her forehead, as though adding pressure would counteract the splitting pain. "Ryder?"

"Here." He moved to her side and held out a bottle of water. "You need to keep drinking water."

"What…happened?"

He sat on the edge of the bed next to her. "Do you remember anything?"

She shook her head, immediately regretting the action after the room tilted around her. A wave of nausea had her shutting her eyes and holding perfectly still. Ryder's hand gently pressed on her shoulder, pressing her back to a reclined position against the pillows.

"Take your time," he crooned.

She nodded, her eyes still closed. The blissful touch of cool, moist fabric dabbed near her hairline and Fiona nearly whimpered. Tears gathered in the corner of her eyes. "What happened to me, Ryder?"

His weight shifted and his fingers brushed hers, then squeezed lightly. "What's the last thing you remember?"

She couldn't…everything was gone. She remembered arriving at the club. VIP area. Charity flirting with Ryder and then… Nothing.

"I don't remember!"

"Shh, it's okay. You're okay."

"We were at the club and in the booth. And

Charity was there… After that, I have no idea. How is that possible?"

Ryder's fingers continued to trace soft circles on her hand. "You were drugged. Someone slipped something into your drink."

"Why?"

He shook his head. "I don't know yet. They threatened the bartender to make it happen. But it wasn't enough of a dose to hurt you, unless someone took advantage of your…incapacity."

Losing hours of her life was impossible to come to grips with. She felt like it had been five minutes. But the red display on the digital clock across the room clearly said it was almost seven in the morning.

"What happened…after the drug?"

"Andi and I realized the problem pretty quickly and we got you out of the club and brought you home."

She practically melted in relief. "Thank you, Ryder. And then staying by my side all night? You didn't have to do that."

Would she ever be able to stop relying on Ryder? Was this her life now? Hiding behind bodyguards or never going out in public?

She closed her eyes against the bleak thoughts of a future as a prisoner. She was safe. For now, that had to be enough. She reopened them, determined to face things head on.

Ryder scratched his collar. "Actually… After we got you settled here, I went back to the club to find out who did this to you."

She sat upright. "You what?"

"I went back to the club."

"Why would you do that? They could have come after you!" She felt hot all of a sudden, her heart racing as she contemplated all the things that could have happened to her last night, but hadn't because Ryder had been there. And what might happen if he were to leave…or be taken away.

His hand found hers again. "Shh, it's okay. I took Cheno with me. We found out what happened, but it's mostly a dead-end."

"How so? Did he arrest the person who did it?" She hated the hope in her voice.

But Ryder shook his head. "No. Somebody black-mailed the bartender into spiking your drink. He's not behind it though. He didn't even know who you were."

She offered a wry smile. "Should I be offended that the man who gave me a roofie didn't even know me?"

A pained expression crossed Ryder's face. "Don't do that. This isn't funny, Fi."

"If I don't laugh, I'll cry. And I'm tired of crying." She sucked in a breath, fighting the tears. "Why is this happening to me?"

"I don't know…but I'm going to protect you." She leaned into his hand as he cupped her cheek.

"Thank you," she whispered.

He dropped his hand and she opened her eyes. His eyes swirled with something, his expression set somewhere between concern and anguish.

"I'm okay," she said quietly. "Thanks to you."

He shook his head. "I wish I would have caught it before you drank it. You didn't deserve this."

Before she could think of a response to his misplaced guilt, he stood and said, "I'll be in the kitchen if you need me."

As he walked away, her heart squeezed tighter at the realization that without Ryder, she could have died three times now. As much as she'd fought his presence in her life, she now understood why Flint trusted him so much.

Ryder McClain was intense. Loyal. And he never pretended to be something he wasn't. Which meant all his tender words and sweet touches? They meant something. And it was high time she let him know that she felt the same.

———

Whatever the mastermind behind the drugging had hoped to accomplish, they'd officially managed to drag his name through the mud. And Fiona's by association.

Ryder scowled at the photos side by side on the front page. One was of him whispering in Charity's ear, and the other was of Fiona wrapped around him as they danced their way out of the club. He was grateful she appeared happy, as opposed to completely out of it like he knew she was at the time.

He, on the other hand, looked like a reckless playboy.

Andi stepped into the kitchen, a shake in hand, still slightly sweaty from her morning run in the cold. How she ran when it was thirty degrees was beyond him.

"Did you grab these?" he asked.

She nodded. "Yeah. Saw them on my run. Figured you'd rather see them early."

He grunted. He'd rather not see them at all. Meaning they wouldn't exist. Judging by the last time they'd been in the papers, Fiona wouldn't be thrilled about the feature.

Andi shrugged. "Sorry. I'm going to grab a shower."

Ryder lifted his coffee cup in acknowledgement. He was incredibly grateful for Andi's help. With the rest of the team still tied up on the Mexico job, he needed the extra hands. She had to leave tomorrow, though. Something about a fundraiser appearance with her sister who was married to the vice president. Guess you don't get to cancel plans on the Second Lady of the United States.

He grabbed his mug and took a deep drink, regretting it when he realized it was still piping hot. Fiona sauntered into the kitchen, the fresh scent of her lavender shampoo trailing behind her. "Feeling better?"

She smiled warmly. "So much better."

"I think maybe you should stay home another day." He said it gently, hopeful she would agree but realized that was unlikely.

As expected, Fiona shook her head. "No, I can't. Tomorrow is the dress rehearsal for *Date Night America*. There is so much to do."

He cleared his throat and waited until she looked

back at him. He moved his eyes to the tabloids. "You might want to look at those then."

Her brow furrowed and she changed direction. Instead of heading to the coffeemaker, she picked up the paper and rolled her eyes.

Ryder grabbed her favorite cup from the cupboard, a heavy pink one with a Bible verse on it. He poured her coffee and crossed the kitchen to set it next to her on the counter as she scanned the article.

"What a joke," she said.

He raised his eyebrows. "You're not upset?" He leaned on the counter beside her.

Fiona turned slightly so she faced him. She looked up at him and he saw the serious expression on her face. "No. I mean, I'm not thrilled that they are spreading lies about me. But I know it's not your fault."

He bit the inside of his lip. That was good, but not exactly what he was hoping to hear. "Okay?"

She slipped a hand around his waist, his breath catching at the intimate contact. "Besides, they got it half right. I am rather smitten with my bodyguard."

He grinned at her admission. "Oh yeah?"

"Mm-hmm. You see, he's strong and brave and kind. And he makes me coffee." She winked with the last statement.

He chuckled. "Ah, priorities." He kissed her gently, savoring the sensation he'd been hoping to repeat for an entire week. "You sure you're okay that people know about…us?"

She nodded. "Yeah, I am. I don't know what 'us' is yet, but you're a good man, Ryder. I'd be a fool not to see it. They can say what they want. We're a team, right?"

Joy spread and filled every dark corner of his broody soul. He wrapped his arms around her waist and pulled her to himself. No matter what happened next, she trusted him.

And she wasn't ashamed to be with him.

For now, that was enough. They could worry about the future later. For now, he just needed to make sure she was safe so there could *be* a future.

CHAPTER TWENTY

THE VALENTINE'S Day dinner special set was everything she'd hoped. Small bistro tables were candlelit just off the main stage, where she could interact with the guest. Tomorrow, anyway. Today was just a dress rehearsal, and the only person who sat at one of the romantic tables for two was Ryder.

She could feel his eyes on her as she moved around the stage kitchen. It was huge, with three different cooking areas and a decoration station and dining table for her to use.

The script they'd created with the menu she'd provided was cheesy but cute.

"They say the way to a man's heart is through his stomach, right? Well, in my experience, that's the way to anyone's heart! So, no matter who you are cooking for this Valentine's Day, stay tuned for some perfect ideas about what to fix for dinner and dessert. And how to decorate."

She smiled broadly at the camera.

The director spoke to the room. "Okay, first commercial break is a short one. Two minutes. Start the clock and everyone on my mark. Three, two, one, set."

A flurry of activity sprang into motion around her as assistants and stagehands poured in from the wings to set up her first segment. Carefully measured bowls of ingredients were rolled in on carts and placed on the counter top, along with the things for a Valentine's Day punch.

The director counted down and the stage cleared, except for her.

"Welcome back. You know, my Nonna was married to my grandfather for nearly seventy years. They both died in their nineties. And Nonna's motto was 'Dessert first,' so that's exactly what we're going to do. Afterall, who can argue with Nonna?"

Here was the awkward part, at least for rehearsal. "Now, as you can see, I've got some friends in the audience. What city are we in, friends?"

Ryder's voice came from the left. "New York City."

"That's right. The Big Apple. Which is why we are whipping up a classic New York cheesecake. The best thing about this is that you can customize it however you or your special someone like. We'll start with the base."

She walked through the preparation of the cheesecake, then grabbed the pie dish to place it in the oven.

"Now, here's the thing about cheesecake. You don't get to throw this in the oven right before your date. It'll take about seventy minutes in the oven, plus another hour to cool, then about four hours in the fridge. So make this early in the afternoon before your date. I'm going to stick this one in the oven, but I've got another one in the fridge. We'll use it later when we plate and top our cheesecake after dinner…"

She leaned to open the oven door, her nose wrinkling at the smell. She looked toward the stagehand off set, even as she swung the door open. Was that–

Then, her world was a flash of orange heat and she was lifted off her feet, her body slamming into the cabinets behind the stove. A chemical smell singed her nose and lungs. Fiona scrambled, crawling and clawing her way along the cabinets. One thought only: get away.

———

His heart stopped, as all the air in the room suddenly disappeared with a deafening blast. Ryder staggered toward the counter Fiona had been standing behind. Before the fireball had engulfed her.

A gauzy haze of smoke filled the room and burned his eyes. "Fiona!" he shouted over the various screams and shouts of the production staff.

"Ryder?"

Relief flooded him at the sound of her voice. He spotted the bright red of her blouse, near the floor toward the edge of the stage to his left. He sprinted to her, wrapping her in his arms. Then he ran his hands down each limb, assessing for injuries.

"Over here! I've got her." He slipped his arm under her knees and arms, carrying her away from the kitchen. He didn't know exactly what had happened, but his first plan was to get her far away from whatever caused that explosion.

He supposed he should be grateful she wasn't hurt worse. He knew from experience that an explosion could be enough to level a building.

The director came over. "Ms. Raven. Are you okay? I can't believe–"

"What on earth happened back there? Is this the kind of operation you run around here?" he snapped at the director in frustration.

"I smelled gas," Fiona said. "And put me down. I'm perfectly capable of walking."

Ryder shook his head and continued carrying her.

"You think it was a gas leak?" Director Roberts asked.

They were almost to the stairs, where he would proceed to carry her down every last flight of them and back to the safety of her apartment. Or maybe Cheno's apartment, so they wouldn't know where to find them.

"I'm not sure. I just know that I– Ryder Michael McClain, put me down right now!"

Ryder spotted an empty conference room and brought her inside, Director Roberts trailing in after them. He shut the door with his foot before setting her down, leaving half a dozen assistants complaining about being stuck in the hallway.

Ryder leaned against the door and crossed his arms. "We need to get out of here, Fiona."

Director Roberts chimed in, "Now there is no need to be hasty. The set is basically fine. We'll have someone replace the stove…"

Fiona nodded. "It could have been a perfectly innocent accident. We don't know what happened."

"Exactly! We don't know what happened. Which is why we have to assume the worst–that it was a direct attack and proceed accordingly." He gestured to the door. "Let's go."

Fiona worried her lip between her teeth, and Ryder softened his tone. "I just want to take care of you, Fi. You know that, right?"

"I know. But, Ryder… This is important. This is my big break into network television."

He saw the glimmer of hope still lingering in her eyes. How it hadn't been extinguished by the exploding ball of fire in the kitchen was beyond him. "You'll get another shot…" he offered, but he knew even before she started to shake her head that it was a long shot.

"I barely got *this* shot. I have to make this happen. I'm fine. Nobody is hurt. And you heard the director— the set is fine. Just bad timing for an oven malfunction."

There was a sick feeling in his gut. Was it just his own overactive imagination? He wished once again that he wasn't the one running point on this. Let it be someone else's call. More importantly, let someone else be the bad guy to Fiona. Because how could he look at the woman he felt so strongly about and crush her hopes and dreams by refusing to let her do the show?

He rubbed the bridge of his nose, pressing back a

headache he wasn't sure was from the stress or the blast. "I need to talk to Raven. Flint," he clarified. "If he approves it, we can move forward."

Later, he stood on Fiona's balcony, talking to her brother. But the news wasn't good. "Things are complicated down here at the border. We won't be back for a few more days. Can't Fiona just postpone this thing?"

"It's a live television special on a major network, Rave." Why did it sound like he was defending Fiona's decision?

"I take it that's a no?"

"Yeah, that's a no." He sighed. "I can put my foot down and tell her no, but I really don't want to disappoint her like that."

There was silence on the other end of the line. "Should I ask why you're so worried about disappointing my sister?"

Heat rose in his cheeks as Ryder stammered. "Uh, um, I–"

Then he heard laughter from the phone call. "It's all good, Ry. I saw you two at my wedding. I may be dense sometimes, but I'm still a genius. And this wasn't rocket science."

"So you…knew?" Well, that was embarrassing.

"I figured there were some feelings there and that

maybe a little extra time together would help you two admit them to each other."

Ryder rolled his eyes. Flint was actually trying to play matchmaker? "And warning me away from her before I came up here?"

"That? Come on, I'm her big brother. It's my job to scare off potential suitors. Even the ones I like."

He shook his head. "You're the worst best friend, you know that?"

"Yeah, yeah. What are we going to do?"

"You won't be back in time?" Ryder knew the answer but still hoped it would be different if he asked again.

"Not even close."

Ryder watched the traffic, tiny vehicles below. In the dark, the blue and red flashing lights of a police car sped through an intersection. "Actually, I've got an idea."

CHAPTER TWENTY-ONE

FIONA PACED the kitchen in her condo, flipping through recipe cards and rehearsing her script. The Valentine's Dinner special was tomorrow, and despite the event nearly being canceled, the show would go on. After maintenance had confirmed the explosion had been a simple gas leak due to a faulty igniter in the oven, Fiona had been even more relieved she didn't let it scare her into backing out.

This was her moment to shine and she wasn't going to let it go that easily.

She flipped to the next notecard as strong arms came around her waist. She leaned back into Ryder's strong frame, enjoying the solid support he provided. He kissed her cheek and murmured, "It's getting late."

He wasn't wrong. Her muscles screamed to sit after another day on her feet and the bruises she carried from her short flight across the kitchen from the blast.

She giggled and shied away from the rough rasp of his stubble on her neck. "Where's Gabbi?"

"She's in her room, safely tucked in with Netflix and a bowl of popcorn."

"Thanks for taking care of her. Of us," she amended.

"That's my job." He spun her around until they faced each other. "Plus, Gabbi seems to think I have a crush on her roommate, and she tells me all the good stories."

Fiona's mouth fell open. "She does not!"

Ryder smiled. "Oh, she does. But it's okay. I think you're cute."

Fiona set her cue cards on the counter behind her so her hands were free to wrap around Ryder's waist. He rubbed her back and she laid her head on his chest.

"Are you ready for tomorrow?" His voice was soft. He was curious, but kind.

She nodded. "I think so. It feels weird that it is finally here. I've been looking forward to it since Christmas. I just want everything to be perfect."

And wasn't that the story of her life? All the pressure, all the expectations. Some of it was from others, but a lot of it was just her and her desire for perfection.

"You'll be great, Fi. But you know something? Perfection is overrated."

She tipped her head up to meet his eyes. "That's where you're wrong. By definition, perfection cannot be overrated."

"Yeah, well. I disagree. Perfection would mean that you lost the little freckle on your ear, or this scar on your shoulder." His fingers traced the destinations his words mentioned, trailing from her ear, down her neck to find a little scar on her shoulder leftover from a biopsy she'd had as a child.

She hummed her approval of his touch, then shook her head at his words. "That's not exactly what I meant."

"What did you mean?" His gentle touch turned into a shoulder massage and Fiona nearly moaned. He gently guided her to the couch as he rubbed her tight muscles.

"Wanting everything to go perfect means that I don't let anyone down. All the people I work with… They work hard to make sure our magazine, our show, our food is everything people expect. Which means, I can't go out there and screw it up. You said it yourself, I'm the face of the company. And messing up means embarrassing myself–and my company. I don't want to do that." Again, she added silently.

"Mistakes are bound to happen though, right? They aren't the end of the world."

"Sometimes, they are, though! Sometimes, mistakes ruin everything and close doors you wish would have stayed open. Maybe every now and then you get lucky and a mistake slips under the radar. But I can't take that risk any more than you can."

"So…what mistake did you make?"

She tensed, frozen under his massaging fingers. "What?"

"This fear of making mistakes didn't just appear out of nowhere. What mistake did you make that is pushing you to perfection now, even if it kills you?"

"I've always been this way. I just like to do things right."

"Maybe so. Flint tells me you've always been an overachiever. But even he says you've taken your fear of mistakes to a different level."

"Great, so now you guys are talking about me?" She hid her discomfort at the question by lashing out. He wasn't wrong. There was a mistake in her past, one that she would never forget. And now this lawsuit was just another reminder of what happened when she didn't keep her guard up.

"It's not like that," he said gently, diffusing her irritation. "I just want to understand what makes you tick. Let me in, Fiona."

She tensed. He wanted to know her mistake. As if there had been only one. She thought about telling him everything. The confession about her lapse early on in her career was on the tip of her tongue. It had led to the current situation and the threat. But she couldn't.

Instead, she thought about before. Even then, when she'd put her trust in her lawyers, it had been because she was so preoccupied making sure every detail of her magazine was perfect, even in the midst of grieving for her mother. That drive for perfection had started long before.

His fingers began to move again and she relaxed. "I was always expected to be perfect. I loved my parents," she said sadly. She missed them every day. "But it was a lot of pressure. Flint was a genius, clearly going to change the world. And I was the bubbly, well-behaved daughter they showed off to their friends."

"It was hard being Ross's little brother... I can't imagine being Flint's."

She shrugged. "It is what it is. But I learned to excel at things quickly."

"So why the fear? It seems like you excel at everything you do."

She scoffed. "It turns out being good *most* of the time isn't good enough. One slip is all it takes to lose everything. One of my favorite professors was in charge of a competition in culinary school. Winner got an internship in Paris. He actually encouraged me to compete," she said wistfully. "And I wanted it so badly." She could hear the pitiful whine of her own voice and shook her head.

"What happened?"

She swallowed and strengthened her tone. "I'm still not completely sure. I made a mistake and my dish…"

She could still remember the laughter at her expense. She shook her head to clear the bad memories. "Chef Glenn was brutal. He berated me and mocked my dish during the judging. The entire class watched me crash and burn, get torn to shreds by my favorite teacher, and they absolutely relished the chance to see me fail. Not to mention the panel of judges–basically every big chef who hired staff members out of the program. In an instant, everyone turned against me." She sagged. "I was a pariah."

Ryder shook his head. "What a jerk."

"I think he was embarrassed because he had nominated me. Needless to say, I did not get that internship in Paris. Chef also pulled the recommendations he'd given for a few other positions as well." She exhaled. "I spent almost two years regaining his confidence enough to land a recommendation for Casa di Milano, my first five-star restaurant. I made sure I never made a mistake for Chef Milano. Or since. I didn't want anyone to have any reason to doubt me."

"No mistakes."

She nodded firmly. "No mistakes."

He leaned forward, and then his lips pressed against her temple. "I'm sorry you have felt like you needed to be perfect for people to like you or your work. I'm not sure I'll ever be able to convince you that isn't the case. But I wish I could. Because going through life on a tightrope, trying never to drop a ball, sounds exhausting."

She was facing him now, his dark-brown eyes warm and inviting. "It can be," she admitted.

"I don't expect you to be perfect," he said. "Because I'm hopelessly in love with the Fiona Raven who makes flawless crème brûlée *and* the Fiona Raven who forgets she's already had dinner and orders an entire second meal. Perfect isn't nearly as fun. I just want you to be you. Mistakes and all."

"I make mistakes sometimes," she said with a smile.

"Oh yeah, like what?"

"Like not doing this more." She leaned in and kissed him. After a moment's hesitation, he responded in kind. His lips were soft and warm under hers and his spicy scent surrounded her. The kiss made her want to curl up in a luxurious blanket of sensations. Physical, yes–there was heat and softness and butterflies.

But even more so, there was vulnerability and acceptance and adoration and relief. Being wrapped in Ryder's embrace felt like eating a bowl of Nonna's *ribollita.* Not only was it deliciously warm and comforting, but it meant she was with someone who knew her and loved her. His hands moved up her neck to her jawline and he cradled her head tenderly. She hummed her approval and deepened the kiss for a moment before pulling back.

Fiona had successfully ignored her own loneliness for a long time. But just like someone starving who suddenly remembered how a full stomach felt, she wasn't sure she would be willing to go back to being alone.

And that was scary. Because as much as Ryder claimed he didn't want perfection, Fiona saw the way he watched her–a mix of awe and attraction–when she was working. He'd told her multiple times how impressed he was with how she balanced all the commitments.

He might say he wanted her imperfections. But he'd never really seen them. So how could he know?

TWENTY-TWO

RYDER HAD CALLED in every favor he was owed, and the presence of the uniformed NYPD officers working security for the live taping of the *Date Night America* Valentine's Day special was evidence that perhaps he had more friends here than he thought. Or at least Cheno did.

They'd screened every person in the audience for weapons, as well as the staff. Nothing to be concerned about.

Cheno walked up to him and Ryder shook his friend's hand. The studio audience was getting settled in their seats, including the special tables at the front of the stage who would interact with Fiona during the show.

"I can't thank you enough, man."

"Absolutely. I know you left under rocky circumstances, but we've still got your back."

Ryder wasn't sure about that. He felt like Cheno had his back, and the man had proved it several times since their chance encounter after Gabbi was hit. But the rest of the NYPD? Ryder wasn't foolish enough to believe they'd come running to help.

"Same goes," he affirmed. "I'm going to run back and check on Fiona again. You've got everything you need here, right?"

Cheno nodded. "Yep. I've got five officers in here, plus the ones outside the studio."

Ryder headed away from the audience and flashed his security pass for the officer guarding the door to backstage.

He found Fiona's dressing room. He could see her reflection in the mirror, surrounded by bright lights. She smiled at him as a makeup artist swiped at her face with a giant poofy makeup brush.

"Is this a bad time?"

Fiona shook her head. "No, I think we're about done, right?"

In moments, the three assistants who'd crowded around her packed their gear and disappeared out of the room.

"You look beautiful," he offered, pressing his

hands into the pockets of his leather jacket.

"Thanks."

"Nervous?"

She shook her head. "Nope. I've got my part down. And I'm trusting you to keep me safe. What do I have to be nervous about?"

Her trust made him smile. She had such faith in his abilities. He had been praying it wasn't misplaced. "I'll be glad when this is all over and I can whisk you somewhere no one can touch you."

She stood and made her way over to him. She circled her arms around his neck, and his hands instinctively found their way around her waist. "Anywhere in particular?"

"Hmmm. Cabo? I bet you look great in a bikini, and I'm tired of the cold."

She giggled. "I could definitely go for a chair on the beach."

He kissed her firmly. "Then let's finish today and make that happen." The threat of the stalker was still out there, but maybe a vacation would give them both a break from the stress of the last month.

An assistant poked their head in the door of the dressing room. "Three minutes to set, Ms. Raven."

She stepped back and brushed her hands down the front of her blouse. "I guess I should head out there."

He placed his hands on hers to still her primping. "You look perfect."

She smiled and pressed onto her toes for a kiss. "Thanks."

"You're going to do awesome. I got your back."

———

Fiona said a quick prayer as she headed toward the set. There were fifteen minutes scheduled ahead of the show start for her to chat with the audience and warm them up. Then, it was showtime.

Applause sounded when she came from backstage. The grin that spread across her face was one-hundred-percent genuine. How could you not smile when a hundred people were cheering for you?

She waved as she stepped to the front of the stage, where a set of assistants adjusted her mic and hair again. When the applause died down, she laughed and spoke to the crowd. "Wow! Save some of that for the cameras, all right?"

Chuckles filtered through the room.

"I am so excited to hang out with you tonight. It might be a little awkward with some of these cameras zooming around. These guys can be a bit intrusive, but try your best to ignore them, okay? We've got about ten minutes until I come back on and do the official version of this greeting, but why don't we just chat a bit first. Who is from New York?"

Fiona led the back and forth with the audience, cracking jokes and getting to know the crowd, especially the couples seated at the tables.

"How long have you been married?" she asked an older couple sitting stage right.

"Thirty-three years," they answered in unison.

"That's amazing. What's your secret?"

The husband turned to his wife, who got a sweet smile on her face. "No secrets. Just try to give more than you get. If you both do that…you'll be in good shape."

Fiona felt the lump in her throat and she searched for Ryder, finding him in the shadows beside the seats. He certainly knew how to give and serve. Did she?

She cleared her throat. "Great advice. Do you mind if I ask you this again while we are live?"

The couple agreed, and then it was time. She stepped back offstage and the director counted down. On television sets across the country, she knew a romantic intro video would be playing with shots of delicious food, candlelit dinners, and celebrity couples giving quotes about love.

Then, the voice-over rang through the studio, announcing her as their host. She walked on stage again, the applause seeming even louder this time.

Showtime.

———

Ryder watched in amazement as Fiona worked the crowd and the ingredients. It both felt like she was hosting a small dinner party and teaching a fancy cooking class at the same time. Whoever had planned the television special had done an amazing job, and segments with musicians performing and celebrity couples toasting to Valentine's Day were sprinkled in. But the focus was on Fiona and the elegant Valentine's dinner she was creating.

The crowd played perfectly into her hand, laughing at her jokes and answering her questions as she cooked. Ryder held his breath while she opened the stove to put the cheesecake inside, but it was uneventful.

She served the soup – something she called *ribollita* – to the couples at the front tables with the help of the stagehands.

"Ah, here we go. What do you think? Doesn't it smell fantastic?"

The young couple nodded enthusiastically and picked up their forks as the camera zoomed in close. Ryder was just grateful he wasn't going to be on camera.

The cameraman panned from the row of tables enjoying their first course back to Fiona, who seamlessly transitioned into a segment from Michael Bublé. Stagehands dressed in black discreetly waited on the tables, filling water glasses and clearing the dishes.

Ryder checked his watch. Forty-five minutes down and another seventy-five to go.

Thirty minutes later, Ryder noticed the sweet older couple Fiona had chatted with before the show acting quite strange. They were whispering to each other, and the man held his head in his hands.

Fiona was chatting about the risotto she was making. But his attention was on the audience.

"The secret to a good risotto is to use broth that is hot, but not boiling. Just below a simmer, so it neither evaporates nor cools down the risotto as you add…"

The various couples were whispering and fidgeting. And Fiona had noticed.

She stumbled. "As you add the stock one ladle at a—"

A loud moan came from stage left, and a young

woman stood up from her chair, making a beeline to the exit. She made it two steps before losing her soup on the polished floor of the studio.

Ryder immediately looked back at Fiona, who was watching in horror. Within moments, the entire row of people she'd been feeding for one hour doubled over in pain or deposited the contents of their stomach on their table.

Fiona stammered. "I think we better cut to a quick commercial break." Her improvised transition was punctuated by the low moans of the audience members. "We'll be right back with more risotto tips and a special message from Poppy Coulter, the Second Lady of the United States and farm-to-table expert."

Director Roberts called time, and Ryder watched as she ran toward backstage, hands on her face.

"Cheno, get these people some medical attention!" he called.

Director Roberts was busy clearing the stage of the sick audience members, but he pointed at Ryder as he helped a woman toward the exit. "We need Fiona back here." Ryder nodded, but Roberts had already moved on, issuing commands to the rest of the audience. "You twelve, I need you to come sit at these tables."

Ryder made a face at the response of the crowd. He couldn't exactly blame them. Nobody wanted to volunteer to eat a meal that had already made a dozen people violently ill. Whatever mistake Fiona had made…it was a doozy.

He remembered her story of public humiliation. A small competition at culinary school was nothing compared to something like this—live on national television.

She had to be absolutely horrified. Ryder headed backstage with a nod at the security guard at the entrance. He found Fiona's dressing room and knocked. "Fiona…sweetheart? Are you okay?"

There was a long pause. "Go away, Ryder," she called.

His brow furrowed. "I just want to talk to you. Everything is going to be okay…"

"It's fine. I just need a minute alone. Can you tell Director Flint that I'll be right there?"

Ryder sighed in resignation. Apparently, she was fine. And she didn't need him. He headed back out to the main studio and flagged down Director Roberts. Then, he paused midstep.

What had Fiona said? He replayed the conversation. She'd said Director Flint. He was sure of it. His eyes widened and he yelled, "Cheno!"

CHAPTER TWENTY-THREE

FIONA BREATHED SLOWLY, trying to remain calm. The man across from her gestured toward the couch with the gun trained on her.

"Sit." The man's mouth was set in a hard line and left no room for argument.

Fiona obeyed. She'd been terrified that Ryder was going to come barging into her dressing room. An act that would have surely ended with one or both of them in the morgue. She just hoped her little signal was enough for him to understand what was happening.

"Please, I don't–"

"Shut up!"

Fiona pressed her lips together.

She kept her eyes on him while he paced the

room. And Fiona prayed. She debated speaking again. Was it worth rattling him? She didn't recognize the man in front of her. His jacket hung limply on his skinny frame, his hair long and unkempt. His cheeks were sunken, and dark circles were like bruises under his eyes.

But under his jacket, he wore the uniform of a stagehand.

She worked hard to keep her tone gentle and non-threatening. "Why are we here?"

He snarled in disgust. "I would have thought you'd have figured it out by now, Ms. Raven. Haven't I given you enough clues? Or are the people you hurt really that unimportant to you? Even after the email with the evidence, you just go on about your life and people think you're so perfect."

She just needed to keep him talking long enough for Ryder to intervene.

"I'm not perfect," she said, opening the dialogue.

———

"Are you sure? Maybe she just misspoke?"

Ryder shook his head. "No way. Fiona doesn't misspeak. It's kind of her thing. Trust me. There is something going on in there."

Director Roberts appeared in the hallway. "Where is Fiona? We need her to continue!"

He grabbed the man around the shoulders and led him away from backstage. "We've got bigger problems. Fiona is being held hostage in her dressing room. I don't care what you need for your show, but you're going to have to continue without Fiona. Got it?"

Roberts swore like a sailor and started yelling at his assistants.

Ryder let Chenoweth call in the SWAT team and slid down to the floor against the wall in the hallway. How had he missed this? All the safeguards in place and someone had managed to get into her dressing room? Apparently, he was in the wrong business. Perhaps they'd been right to kick him from the SWAT team. And Flint would be right to kick him from Black Tower after this. If anything happened to Fiona, he knew her brother would never forgive him. Which didn't really matter, considering he knew he would never forgive himself.

SWAT was at least twelve minutes out, unless their response time had improved since he was on the force. He pulled out his phone and made the hard call.

"Flint, we've got a problem."

His friend's voice was concerned. "I've got the

show on. What happened? And why isn't Fiona back on air?"

Ryder told him about the food poisoning and now being held backstage.

"Are you sure it was food poisoning?"

"Sure seemed like it. They were throwing up all over the place."

"You think it was an accident? That doesn't sound like Fiona."

Ryder considered the theory. Flint was right. It didn't sound like Fiona. "I don't know, man! What does it matter? She's trapped in there with a crazy person, and if I barge in there, who knows what he'll do?"

Flint yelled, "Ryder McClain, get out of your head and do your job! Got it?"

Ryder sucked in a surprised breath. "SWAT is on the way. We'll get her."

Flint cursed. "Forget SWAT. Trust your gut. Figure out who did this and how to get her out. Got it?"

"Yes, sir."

Ryder hung up the call and immediately dialed Joey.

Joey's tone was agitated. "I'm on a date, Mac."

"Well, it's canceled. We've got an emergency."

In an instant, Joey was all business. "I'm on it. What do you need?"

"I'm going to send you photos of every person who could be involved. I need positive IDs on every single one of them." He knew it was a hard ask, but he always counted on Joey and her incomparable skills in the clutch.

"It'll take me five minutes to set up," she said firmly.

"You've got three."

Ryder jogged to the control room where all the camera feeds were displayed on screens. It looked like they were looping various celebrity interviews.

He raised his hands and spoke over the buzz of the room. "I need every camera angle from the first half of the show. Anything near the food or the tables where the people got sick."

Blank faces stared back at him.

"Now!" he barked.

A young woman in thick-framed glasses slid her seat back. "Here, you can use my station."

He sat down, and she leaned over his shoulder to pull the footage up. He watched in double speed, focusing on the footage that wasn't used in the show. He paused as a stagehand came near the food.

"How do I take a picture?"

She showed him, and he snapped the screenshot, then sent it to Joey, repeating every time a new face came on.

When he came to the camera trained on the tables, he leaned closer. A scrawny man in black waited on the tables, refilling their waters. He saw him slip his hand into his pocket, but the video was too dark to see exactly what happened. Could he have drugged their drinks?

As crazy as it seemed, that would explain it. There was no way Fiona made a mistake that severe. Not that it would be any consolation after the maniac killed her.

He followed the path of that worker with the cameras until he had a clear shot of his face. Then he sent it to Joey along with a message that this suspect took priority.

Maybe if he could get enough background on the stalker, he could figure out why he was targeting Fiona and how to stop him. At least he prayed that would be the case.

———

Fiona thought about every move carefully, trying to anticipate how the man would react. He was waiting for something. But she didn't know what.

"Please, I'd like to understand. Tell me what I missing."

"You really don't get it do you? I've lost everything, and it is your fault. When she told me she could help me get revenge, I jumped at the chance."

Fiona's mind raced. Who was he talking about? "Who said that?"

"Oh, she thought she was so smart"—he tapped his head with his finger—"meeting me at that other office. But I recognized her. I should have known better than to trust a politician." He continued ranting about how he was finally going to get revenge.

Her phone was across the room, and Fiona desperately wished she could get to it. Instead, she tried to keep him talking.

"Tell me. Revenge for what? What did I do? I want to make it right. "

He scoffed. "You can't make it right! My son is dead because of you! And pretty soon you will meet the same fate, thanks to her. But not until I do what I came to accomplish. Killing you would be too easy. Ruining your business and your reputation, though? That's what really needs to happen. She just needs to stay out of my way. Her and her precious Syndicate have been more disruptive than I imagined. I should have told her to keep her money."

Fiona's fingers itched, wishing for her phone. The Syndicate? She'd heard about them from Flint and Jessica. What did they want with her, though?

He continued, "I was going to embarrass you, get pictures with you and that security guard. Start rumors swirling. And if he had not intervened at the club, you would've made a fool of yourself there too. I had it all figured out. The poisoning of the people at this event was going to be the last straw. Just a few conveniently tipped reporters to sell their story of your fall from grace.

Fiona tried to process everything he just told her. What had been him and what had been The Syndicate started to blur. "The notes?"

"That was me. Hoping I could rattle you."

"How did you get past security? The cameras?"

He waved a hand, like it was no big deal. "A few tricks from my former employer."

Fiona nodded as though she understood. "What about Gabbi? The van?"

He shook his head. "They probably only wanted me involved to get close to you and throw you off the track. Probably so I could be the patsy when it all went down. Morris got jumpy, and her people tried to take you out instead. Decided to send in someone else. The van. The shooter at Times Square. But not anymore. If I'm going down for your murder, then maybe I'll just do it myself."

She paled, remembering the fear of ducking from the bullets as they flew through the Square. "But the blackmail note was you. And the tabloids? What about my oven? The explosion?"

He clenched his fist. "It was just supposed to sabotage your dish. Throw you off your game." He chuckled. "I almost thought you were going to cancel the event. But I'm glad you didn't." He gestured to the hallway. "The entire world is out there. The studio is scrambling to cover for you, and the rest of the world is wondering what just happened to the perfect Fiona Raven. Embarrassed on national TV. You gave food poisoning to a dozen people." He clicked his tongue in admonishment. "Shame, shame."

Fiona felt her heart drop. "But I didn't!"

He laughed—a dark, sinister sound that made the hair stand up on her neck.

"Do you think that matters? You're more naïve than I thought. Once they see the cover-up, how you and your company poisoned six people and paid them hush money to keep it quiet, you'll be ruined."

It was all starting to come together. The blackmail

evidence, stolen from her file room and turning up in her inbox. This had to tie back to that.

"You mentioned…your son?" She asked the question gingerly, not wanting to upset him.

Emotion crossed his face, turning it from sneer into a crumpled visage of sorrow. "Lucas was only five. He was perfect. And he loved your chicken alfredo."

Fiona felt the knot twist tighter in her stomach. She knew where this was going.

"I'm so sorry. I didn't know!" But was it was probably pointless. Why would he believe her? "I should've known. I should've paid attention. I'm so sorry about your son. You have every right to be angry."

"Don't placate me! You don't have any idea what it is like to lose a child. To some freak accident. An undercooked piece of chicken?" He cursed. "No. You don't get to apologize. This is your fault. And you will pay."

CHAPTER
TWENTY-FOUR

"YOU BETTER HAVE something for me, Joey."

"I'll never let you down, Mac. Here's the scoop on your boy. His name is Christopher Timperley. Until a few years ago, he was a systems analyst at Pinnacle Tech. A hacker. That explains how he got into the Raven Foods security grid so easily."

"Didn't Pinnacle buy Raven Tech?" Flint Raven's former security tech company had made the rounds in the venture capital world. It was a precarious connection, but it might be relevant.

"Six months ago. After he left."

Ryder nodded. "OK. Then what's his deal?"

"Here's where it gets interesting. His only tie that I could find to Raven Foods is a court filing. The documents are confidential. But it is some sort of settlement."

Ryder frowned. "What does that mean?"

"I'm not exactly sure. My best guess? His son died eighteen months before the settlement. I may have broken a few laws, but I got the medical records. His son died from complications of food poisoning."

Ryder cursed under his breath. At least he had motive. "Tell me about the son."

"Seems like a normal kid. Five years old, played soccer. Hadn't started kindergarten yet. Only child."

"And his mom?"

He heard the sound of a keyboard in the background. Then Joey responded, "Divorced. A few months after the settlement."

"Thanks. I guess it's time for me to go talk down a revenge-seeking father."

"Wait." Joey's tone stopped him in his tracks.

"What is it?"

"I have proof that ties Citadel back to the gang that kidnapped Jessica."

His mouth dropped open. What was Joey saying? "So we know for sure that Citadel is Syndicate?"

"Yes. But we don't know that this attack is necessarily Syndicate related."

Right. His head was spinning. Citadel was

targeting Fiona. That didn't mean Syndicate was targeting her. But he didn't like the odds. "That's a lot of coincidences."

"I know. I'll keep digging. But we haven't seen anything from the Syndicate in three years. Not since Jessica. It took less than forty-eight hours in federal custody for that guy to end up dead. My guess? Someone was more interested in making sure he didn't talk than listening to what he might have to say."

Ryder wanted to punch something. "What am I supposed to do? I've got Fiona trapped back there with a madman. Whether or not he's the one who hired Citadel or some pawn in Syndicate's game, I have to go get her."

"Pretty much. Just be safe. One last thing. I did that double-check on the bartender you asked about."

He swallowed his impatience. This seemed unimportant. "And?"

"Not involved, as far as I can tell. His precious dog, Roxie, missed two days of doggy daycare, but seems to be back now."

"Thanks." He hadn't expected anything, but the thought of the scrawny bartender still made him want to punch him in the goatee. Roxie. What a joke. He ended the call, pressing his fingers into the bridge between his eyes. He needed a plan.

After a moment, he waved Cheno over. "Is SWAT here yet?"

"They just pulled in." Ryder turned to go meet them, but Cheno grabbed his arm. "Wait, you should know…it's Captain Bailey."

Of course it was. He nodded. "Okay." Nothing like the middle of a crisis to face the ghosts of your past.

Ryder met Captain Bailey at the entrance of the studio. "Captain!" he called to get his attention.

"Time for you to leave, McClain. Let the A-Team take it from here."

"With all due respect, sir. That's not gonna happen."

Captain Bailey rolled his eyes, and Ryder bit back the frustrated reply. "I know we have a complicated history, but this is my fight. Fiona Raven is my responsibility. And I have information you need to help save her."

"Let's walk."

Ryder led Captain Bailey and the team into the now-vacated studio space.

"Here's the rundown. Ms. Raven has been the target of a stalker for the last three months. It has escalated from notes designed to elicit fear to black-mail. She was the target of a shooting and a pedestrian hit-and-run. She was also drugged at a party. Tonight, the man spiked the drinks of the audience to make it appear they had been poisoned."

Captain Bailey raised his eyebrows. "Why is this the first we're hearing about it?"

"There were officers on the scene at one of the break-ins and at the pedestrian hit-and-run. I'm sure it simply wasn't *high-priority enough*," he said with a pointed bitterness that hinted at their history. It was a direct quote used to describe events just prior to Ryder being kicked off the force.

The leadership had lost trust in his instincts and ability to remain impartial, after he had comman-deered police resources to follow up on a case that turned out to be nothing serious.

Apparently, Captain Bailey would never forgive him for wasting his time, and Ryder would always have a bit of a problem with authority. Every request for follow-up had been met with those words. Not a high priority.

They said it was just a routine domestic dispute. But it was the beginning of Ryder's doubt in his instincts. Because every fiber of his being told him that there was more going on in that house than what met the eye. And impersonating the commander and calling in the SWAT team? That had been a big breach in protocol.

For the last ten years, Flint and Ross had been trying to convince him that he could trust his instincts. It just seemed like they usually let him down.

"So what's the play? Do you even want us here?" Captain Bailey shrugged. "We can leave."

"No. It's good you're here. My hands are tied operating in the city. I've got my pistol. That's it. This could go a hundred different ways. First things first, we need eyes in that dressing room."

"Agreed." Bailey called over his shoulder to another man in tactical gear. "Ruben, get the snake."

A few minutes later, Bailey, Ryder, and Ruben were looking at a grainy image of the dressing room on a small tablet.

Ryder felt a surge of relief seeing that Fiona was unhurt. But his heart sank at the sight of the pistol being waved carelessly in the grip of Christopher Timperley.

"He's fragile. This is a revenge mission. He lost his son, and he blames Fiona and Raven Foods."

"OK." Bailey nodded. "We can work with that."

As Bailey prepared to make contact, Ryder

watched Timperley pace around the room. He checked his watch. Ryder caught a glimpse of a shadow on the man's hand. The tattoo the bartender had mentioned? It was the right place. Timperley paced some more. What was he waiting for?

His eyes moved to Fiona. She sat unmoving on the couch. Good girl. Stay compliant.

The phone in the dressing room rang. Ryder could hear it through the wall. He watched Timperley jump at the sound and his posture tensed. He kept the gun trained on Fiona as he walked to the phone.

"Christopher Timperley? This is Captain Bailey with the NYPD. How are things going in there?"

———

Fiona shifted on the couch, hoping the distraction of the phone call would keep him busy. She inched toward the end table, where her phone was mostly hidden under a taping schedule.

"I don't want anything. Leave me alone!" He slammed down the receiver.

Fiona stopped her trek across the sofa, sitting perfectly still and hoping he didn't notice the few feet she'd moved while he was on the phone.

She felt the urge to look at her phone again. It

seemed impossible but she kept her gaze on the man. He was pacing again and checking his watch. Muttering under his breath. He pulled a cellphone from his pocket.

She swallowed her fear. "Wh-what are you going to do to me?"

He looked up at her, as though surprised she was still there. His eyes narrowed in anger. Perhaps forcing him to look at her was a bad plan. His loathing was palpable. "Just shut up!" Then he resumed his muttering.

Fiona kept her eyes on him and scooted toward the edge of the couch.

Suddenly, he stopped and spoke clearly. "I've got no choice. They'll kill me if I don't kill you." In three steps, he was in front of her, gun pointed directly at her face.

The blood froze in her veins. "No. There's another way. Tell the police!"

His arm jerked and she squeezed her eyes closed. Pain exploded in her cheek and jaw as she was knocked to the ground. Her hands covered her face. She tasted the blood in her mouth, and her head swirled.

CHAPTER TWENTY-FIVE

HANDS TUGGED on Ryder's shoulders as he scrambled down the hallway. Red-hot rage filled him at the sight of Timperley smacking Fiona across the face with his gun.

There was only one thought now. It consumed him.

Get to Fiona.

He'd break down the door himself. Not even a bullet would stop him.

But Cheno's voice broke through the haze. "She's okay. She's okay. Think, Ryder."

He stared at the door down the hallway, a mere 100 feet away. Fiona was there. "Somebody better sign off on the plan right now, or I'm crashing that door myself."

Bailey's gravelly voice came from his left, along with a heavy hand on his shoulder. "We'll get her, Mac. Let's do this. On my count."

Ryder watched as two unfamiliar officers in tactical gear disappeared up the stairwell. They'd be coming in from the floor above, using the ventilation shaft.

He met Bailey's eyes with a stern gaze. "I'm on the breach team."

Bailey studied him for a moment, then gave a curt nod. "You remember where the gear is?"

Ryder sprinted to the SWAT van, parked just outside the doors. He found a bulletproof vest and helmet.

With a reticent glance at the armory cabinet and the heavy-duty padlock, he felt for his pistol on his hip. It would have to do.

When he went back upstairs, Bailey gave him a head nod. "Still looks good."

"Where is the team?"

"They are about three minutes from entry."

Ryder shook hands with the other SWAT members. Most were new faces, but a couple knew and remembered him. Whether that was a good thing or not, he wasn't sure.

He was third in formation as the team advanced

down the hallway. Fiona was in there. He kept his mind focused on the goal. "I'm coming for you, princess. Stay alive."

————

Fiona winced at the throbbing ache in her jaw. She never thought she'd be grateful to be pistol-whipped. But she'd honestly believed her life was over as the man stood in front of her, gun raised.

Right now, he was as far across the room as he could be, watching her, a look of horror on his face. "Oh God. What have I done? I'm not a killer. I'm sorry, Lucas. Daddy is sorry."

Fiona struggled back on the couch. "It's okay. I'm okay."

He covered his face with his hands and turned toward the wall. Fiona reached for her phone, stifling a groan at the sudden movement.

Her fingers fumbled for the device and finally closed around the slick case, tucking it against her palm. She pulled it close to her hip, still keeping one eye on him.

"You can get out of this. If you turn me over, the police can help you. But you have to let me go!"

Her kidnapper shook his head, his eyes wide and

the circles under them seeming deeper than before. "No. I can't. There's only one way out of this."

Fiona filled with dread as he lifted the gun.

———————

In his earpiece, Bailey's rough tone counted down. Ryder and the team stood silently just outside the dressing room.

"Ten, nine…"

Ryder tapped the barrel of his gun along with the count. He wanted to rush it. Every second counted and they could be too late. But he'd watched every movement Chris Timperley had made in the dressing room. His gut was telling him that the man wasn't a killer. Someone was pulling his strings, turning the heartbroken father into a vindictive stalker.

"Eight. Seven. Six…"

But he'd been horrified after hurting Fiona.

The crack of a gunshot came from within the room and he yelled, jumping out of position to approach the door. One of the SWAT members kicked at the door, and Ryder rushed in behind him, gun raised.

He swept the room from right to left, knowing without a doubt that the officer in front of him was sweeping left to right, and the one behind would start head on. Every muscle was on a hairpin, but the sight of a body on the floor made his heart stop. It wasn't Fiona. Around him, the other officers emerged from the bathroom, and the hallway breach team moved in on Timperley. In two steps he had crossed the room and pulled Fiona into his arms. Everything else faded but the sweet feeling of her in his arms. Alive.

———

Fiona stared straight ahead as Ryder wrapped her in his arms. The carnage of the scene in front of her was impossible to process. She squeezed her eyes shut against it, buried her face in Ryder's shoulder. But the vision of the distraught father turning the gun on himself kept replaying.

"Shh, shh. It's okay. I've got you. You're okay."

Ryder's soothing voice made her realize she was sobbing, her voice crying out in horror and relief and adrenaline-fueled shakes.

"Is he… Is he dead?"

Ryder squeezed. "Yeah, he is."

Distantly, Fiona registered a strong voice calling out in the room. "All clear. Everybody clear out."

She tucked herself against Ryder's strong frame,

wanting nothing more than to melt into him. "I knew you'd keep me safe."

"You were so brave. And clever, with that clue about Flint."

Fiona shuddered. "I thought I was going to die," she cried.

"Shh, shh. It's okay. It's over."

Fiona allowed herself to lean into Ryder. She felt herself shaking, a result of the adrenaline, no doubt. The reality of what had just happened was staring her in the face, the body still on the floor. She didn't know exactly how these things worked, but she was pretty sure someone would be here soon to take it. She needed to pull herself together. She sniffled quietly and wiped her eyes on the sleeve of Ryder's shirt. Then, she pulled her phone from under her hip, where it had been since she discreetly grabbed it without her captor realizing it.

It had been vibrating, quietly but nearly nonstop. As she tapped on the screen, a flurry of alerts greeted her. It was habit more than actual intent that made her click on the social media alert letting her know that she had been tagged in a post.

When the page loaded, her heart sank. How had she forgotten what had happened before? *Before* seemed like an entirely different world. Before the dressing room. Before the hostage situation. Before she'd watched a tortured father take his own life right in front of her.

Yes, before barely registered anymore. But there it was, in brightly colored images on her screen.

Fiona Raven Poisons Twelve on National TV.

Next post.

Is America's Culinary Sweetheart's Career Ruined?

Another post.

Fiona Raven: Culinary Genius or Careless Diva?

She sucked in a shaky breath. She should have seen this coming. Hadn't that been his intention? To ruin her career? How would she ever come back from this? Maybe it wasn't worth trying. She would be a laughing stock, and even if the truth came out, about how someone had sabotaged the special… That would only lead to the explanation of why. And the awful cover-up her lawyers had orchestrated.

A message from Gabbi registered on the top of the screen.

GL: You are still the best in my book.

Fiona dismissed the notification, her attention stuck on hateful comments collecting on the videos. As she stared at the damaging whirlwind of rumors, speculation, and opinion; the phone was gently pulled from her fingers. Ryder slipped it in his pocket and wrapped his arm around her shoulder pulling her back to himself.

"They don't know you. But if they did, they would never think poorly of what happened."

She nodded but knew it wasn't too convincing. In the end, the entire thing was her fault. Her oversight all those years ago.

Ryder continued. "I'm so sorry, Fi. I should have seen him. He poisoned those people. Your show was ruined, but this wasn't your fault. But even if it were, people make mistakes."

"I'm so sorry, Flint. I should have told you. I should have told you everything about the blackmail."

Flint's face sobered. "What do you mean?"

She brushed the tears from her cheeks and looked at the body on the floor for a moment. "Him. The lawsuit. I shouldn't have kept it from you. I was just so ashamed… And his poor child!" She sobbed into his shoulder, waiting for him to push her away.

Instead, he rubbed her shoulder softly and whispered to her. "It's okay, Fi. I wish I'd known, because maybe then I could have stopped this. But it's okay now. We're okay. We offer grace, remember?"

Ryder's sweet words were a balm to her soul.

Gabbi's message replayed in her brain. What had she done to deserve a friend like her? It wasn't because she was perfect. More than anyone, Gabbi knew she wasn't.

Just like Ryder. And yet, they were still by her side.

Could it be that easy? She had never really given herself grace. As much as she believed in God's forgiveness, it had always seemed like it was meant for others. She needed to earn it, just like everything else in her life.

But here was Ryder, who had seen her lie, sneak around, and put on a fake persona of confidence. And he hadn't walked away. Even more surprisingly, she had known even as she stared down the barrel of the gun that Ryder wouldn't give up.

As he rubbed her shoulder and she rested her head on his chest, she realized that being seen as imperfect and still loved was a thousand times better and being viewed as perfect from a distance.

Perhaps it was time to let the world see her up close. Imperfect and messy, but doing her best. And still one heck of a chef.

"Thank you," she said quietly. "I don't know how I'm going to recover from this professionally, but right now, I just know it doesn't really matter, as long as you are by my side."

Ryder shifted slightly so their eyes met. She tipped her face up, offering her lips to his. The kiss was soft and sweet, transforming to urgent and nearly desperate.

"I thought I lost you," he said.

"Never." She sealed the promise with another kiss, and then tucked her head back under his chin. The light pressure of a kiss on the top of her head made her smile.

Then a voice said, "It's time to go. Ms. Raven, we've got a few questions for you."

———

Ryder looked up in confusion. The room was empty, except his friend Cheno, who stood at the door with a hand extended to the hallway.

He helped Fiona to her feet. "Come on, let's get out of here." They walked slowly to the door.

Cheno held out his hand to shake Ryder's. Ryder shook it and looked at his friend. But Cheno's smile didn't reach his eyes. A knot began to form in his gut. It couldn't be.

He forced a smile. "Pretty wild day, right?"

Cheno nodded, but his attention was on Fiona.

"I've been meaning to ask—did you ever follow up with the bartender to see if his dog was okay? What was her name?"

Cheno chuckled. "Roxie. What a freaking pansy that guy was," he said distractedly. "Let's go, Ms. Raven. I'll take you to a conference room."

Betrayal hit hard.

Ryder pushed Fiona behind him, grabbed the gun from his hip, and pointed it at his friend. In an instant, Cheno's gun was pointed at him in return. Ryder's heart sank. Somehow, he'd actually hoped his gut was wrong on this one. But Cheno hadn't heard the name of the dog. Joey had just told him that on the phone.

His friend's face was hard and determined. "Sorry, Mac. I've got to do it. There's too much on the line."

"What are you talking about? What's on the line?"

"I was supposed to get close to you. Report back on your plans. Morris saw that Timperley wasn't going to get things done."

Ryder filed away the name for later and positioned himself between Cheno and Fiona. "But not you, Tim. You're not weak."

Chenoweth flipped the safety on his gun, fixing it and his eyes on Ryder. "Nope. I'm not."

"What's this about?"

"It doesn't matter, Mac. You're not here. You don't care anymore! You've got your new life and your new fancy job in private security. While me and the NYPD do your dirty work. Well, not anymore."

"So what, you're taking down an innocent woman?"

Cheno shook his head, and Ryder saw the flicker in his eyes. Doubt.

"Come on. You're an honorable man. I know you. What are they giving you, man?"

Cheno's eyes fluttered shut, and Ryder made his move. In one step, he pushed the gun skyward while stepping closer. The gun exploded near Ryder's ear as Cheno wrestled him for control. Ryder smashed his wrist against the doorframe and the gun clattered to the floor. Then he shoved his friend across the hallway into the wall on the opposite side. Cheno grabbed for Ryder's gun.

He shoved the tip of the barrel under Cheno's chin, tipping his head into the wall. Cheno froze and a garbled cry cut off.

"You are a disgrace to the badge. I'm ashamed to have ever called you my friend."

Chenoweth closed his eyes. "Just do it. Kill me."

Ryder pressed harder. It was tempting. "Fiona," he

said instead. "Go back into the studio and get Captain Bailey."

He kept his eyes on Cheno, and his gun firmly pressed against the man's throat.

Bailey came back with Fiona. "What the… Stand down, Mac."

Without looking away from his target, he answered, "Can't do that, sir. This man is a traitor. He tried to kill us."

"Something to say, Officer Chenoweth?"

Cheno shook his head tightly, moisture slipping from the corner of his eye.

Bailey swore and sighed, then stepped closer. Ryder released the pressure but kept his gun trained on Cheno as Bailey pulled the man's hands behind his back.

Bailey called two more officers from the studio, who came down the hallway and escorted Cheno away.

"Thanks, Cap."

Bailey nodded. "Yeah. Well, I trust your instincts."

Ryder frowned. "You do?"

"Yeah. There's something I better tell you. Come on, let's walk."

Ryder followed his former boss, tucking Fiona under his arm as they walked.

"After you left… Something happened. I should have told you right away, but I was ashamed. That house you reported. Called SWAT on?"

"The Brightons." Ryder would never forget that call.

Bailey nodded. "Yeah. A year later, neighbors reported suspicious activity in the basement." He shook his head. His voice was tortured when he continued. "The man had four teenage girls locked in a secret room."

Ryder stopped midstep. A small gasp of horror escaped from Fiona.

When he could speak, it was through gritted teeth. "What?"

Bailey exhaled. "I'm saying you were right. Your instincts were solid. The man was a monster and there was something going on. We just couldn't find it. And I didn't trust you enough to dig further. I'm sorry."

Ryder didn't know whether to scream or cry. Those poor girls. He knew he'd heard something! But when SWAT had come back to sweep the house, they hadn't found a trace. And he looked like a paranoid washout who had stepped out of line. He'd trusted his commanding officer to follow through and trust him. And where had it gotten him?

He turned to face Captain Bailey. "I've spent the better part of the last ten years reliving that decision. Questioning my judgment. Disregarding my gut. And you knew this entire time?"

Bailey looked down. "I should have reached out and found a way to let you know. But it was easier to try to forget. But I could never stop thinking of how much longer those girls lived in misery because I was impatient and hasty on that call." Bailey laid a hand on Ryder's shoulder and looked him in the eye. "I'm sorry, Mac. You were a good officer. You're a good man. And if you ever want a spot on the force, you know I'll make it happen."

Ryder nodded. "Thank you, sir. But I don't see that happening anytime soon."

"I understand." Bailey's eyes shifted to Fiona. "Take care of this one," he told her.

"I will."

Ryder watched Bailey walk away, then turned to Fiona. "Taking care of you is my job."

A hint of a smile crossed her face. "Maybe we can take care of each other."

"Yeah. That sounds good."

CHAPTER TWENTY-SIX

APPLAUSE RANG through the small studio as Fiona crossed the stage and greeted Jason Knight, the late-night talk show host. This was her sixth similar appearance on late-night and daytime talk shows. It was no surprise that the world was curious about what had happened. The press conference the following day, complete with her swollen and bruised face, had gone a long way to quelling the rumors about her food poisoning the audience on national TV.

But it wasn't enough. She was determined to tell her story, to let the world in.

"Ms. Raven. Oh, it is so wonderful to have you here."

"Please, call me Fiona. I'm glad to be here."

"You've had quite an exciting few weeks. Tell us what happened.'

"Oh, you mean the upcoming launch of Raven jarred pasta sauces?" she teased. The acquisition of PrimoPak foods had fallen through, but she'd found another processor to purchase instead. They were a better fit anyway. PrimoPak came with some legacy contracts she didn't want to deal with.

Jason laughed. "Well, obviously, we want to hear about that. But first, we all want to know... Did those people get food poisoning? From your cooking?"

"First of all, I feel so bad that those innocent people were hurt because of something that involved me. But the truth is, someone intentionally poisoned them to make me look bad."

"Wow, really? Who would do such a thing and why?"

"That's actually why I wanted to come and share." She crossed her legs. "See, I've been killing myself my entire career to seem perfect. But the truth is, nobody is perfect. Ten years ago, there was an error in manufacturing at my Chicago food plant. I heard about it, and I hired lawyers who assured me that everything was taken care of."

She swallowed. It never got easier to share this part. "I trusted them, and I went about my other business. I didn't ask any more questions and I now consider it my biggest mistake. You see, the man who sabotaged the Valentine's Day special and held me hostage in my dressing room was a victim of that mistake. His son died due to an error at my facility. And I never even knew."

"Is it true that he committed suicide after holding you captive? Why share the rest of this? Afterall, it's been buried for ten years."

"You're right." She held her hands open in front of her. She was done hiding. "It probably would have been easier to carry on. I could let his story die and be buried along with him. But I realized something in that dressing room: I want people to trust me. And if you don't really know me, then there will always be this disconnect. I realize this admission of my own carelessness could cost me customers and fans. But I have to be honest. It's time I was honest with everyone. I'm not perfect. I work really, really hard to do things correctly–to make sure my recipes are flawless and my business runs well."

She looked out over the audience. "But I'm afraid I've been giving the impression that it all comes easily. And that couldn't be further from the truth. I'm just like anyone else. Sometimes," she leaned toward

Jason and stage-whispered, "I even burn my risotto. Don't tell Nonna."

Laughter fluttered through the audience and Jason grinned.

"Not the risotto!"

Fiona leaned back and gave a guilty smile. The hard part was over, and she knew the rest of the interview would be mostly light-hearted banter. Her job was done. After a long week of telling her story and baring her soul, she would be able to put this chapter behind her. Time would tell what the true fallout was. She hadn't wanted to look, but Gabbi assured her that the response to her interviews was overwhelmingly positive. To quote her flamboyant friend: "Now everybody thinks they're your best friend. Pssh, don't they wish!"

After a few more jokes, Jason turned serious. "What's this I hear about being drugged at a party?"

She nodded. "Yes, I was. The same man who took me hostage and sabotaged the special, also slipped something in my drink at a birthday party earlier in the week. I thank God every day that my bodyguard was there to keep me safe. I don't remember anything from that night. It's very disconcerting."

Jason's eyes danced. "Ooh, tell me more about this bodyguard."

Fiona felt the heat rise in her cheeks. This had not been a part of the planned interview. "Well, you know my brother, Flint?"

"Of course. Everyone remembers Flint Raven. Haven't seen him on the eligible bachelor list lately."

"That's because he got married. But, when he heard about my stalker, he sent an old friend to watch out for me. Ryder has done an amazing job."

"And those rumors about the two of you?"

She smiled. "We are taking things one day at a time…but I'm planning on a lot of days with him as more than my bodyguard."

CHAPTER TWENTY-SEVEN

THE NEXT DAY, Ryder walked through the front door of Black Tower Security, his duffel bag tucked under one arm. Dolores, the grandmotherly woman who watched the front door and answered the phones, greeted him.

"Ryder. So good to see you."

Ryder smiled at her. Dolores may appear frail and gentle to the untrained eye, but he knew she'd recently retired from the CIA and could single-handedly protect the entire compound from her desk with her skills and Flint's specialized tech system.

"I saw your young lady on Knight Nightly last week."

Ryder nodded and fought a smile. He grinned every time he thought about that particular interview.

Hearing Fiona confirm their relationship, and hint at a future had been unexpected. Despite her claims immediately following the events of Valentine's Day weekend, he still partly expected her to push him away. Would he ever feel good enough for someone like her?

Plus, there was still the whole living in different places thing. Long distance was fine, short-term. Especially with his crazy schedule at BTS. They never knew where the next job would be. But he wanted to come home to her. He wondered if BTS would be okay if he were based in New York.

Ross greeted him as he stepped through the door from the lobby to the secured area where the team worked. "Hey. It's about time you got back."

He shook his brother's hand. "A few things to take care of before I could leave New York."

Ross gave a knowing smile. "A few things to take care of, huh? Are you sure you just weren't quite ready to say goodbye to a certain someone?"

"Maybe so," he said with a shrug.

"Flint has been waiting to see you," Ross said, clapping a hand on his shoulder and heading the opposite direction.

Ryder would make his way to see his friend, but first he needed to talk to Joey. He wouldn't have been able to do anything the last few weeks without her help. She had identified Chris Timperley, but their work wasn't done yet.

He poked his head into the dark cave that functioned as Joey's office. She resembled a Starship Commander the way the screens surrounded her. Even her office chair looked more like a NASCAR driver seat than a desk chair. It even had lights, and they matched her keyboard.

He shook his head. How someone could spend all day looking at a screen was beyond him. But he couldn't deny the usefulness.

He knocked on the doorframe, but she didn't turn. He knocked louder. Nothing. So, he came around the side of her chair to get her attention. She gasped and her hand flew from the keyboard to her chest. "Dangit, Mac. You scared me half to death."

He winced at her volume and pointed to her headphones, where he could hear the faint rhythm of music.

She pulled the large earmuffs off, and the music became clearer. Was that…Disney music? Joey ran a hand over her unruly curls.

She hit the keyboard a few times and the sound stopped. "Sorry about that. In the zone."

"I can see that."

She grinned. "I got a new toy. Want to see it?"

"Would Ross approve?"

She got a mischievous grin on her face. "Probably not. But it uses traffic cameras to follow license plates and map their routes."

He raised his eyebrows. "Cool."

"I know! Now, what did you need? More info on Morris? I'm pretty sure I gave you everything I have."

"No, it's not that. I've got a plan, but I need a few more days. Keep an eye on her, though?"

Joey nodded, her eyes wide behind the thick-framed glasses. "Yeah. Whatever you need."

Ryder gave an appreciative smile. "Thanks. One last thing. We need to keep this between us for now."

Joey raised an eyebrow. "You sure about this?"

Ryder nodded. "Yeah. I'm going to do everything I can to keep Morris and The Syndicate away from Fiona and Flint and Black Tower." He could tell Joey didn't like that she needed to keep a secret. He smiled slightly. "I'll tell you what—if you ever feel like you need to bring them in, you can. For now, though, can you let me handle it?"

Joey nodded. "I got your back, Ryder."

"Same goes. Always."

Ryder waved goodbye to the spunky hacker, nearly crashing into Tank in the hallway.

"Mac! You're back." The giant man was intimidating as heck and rarely smiled, but Ryder grinned at the relatively warm greeting.

"Good to see you, man. I heard you bought a house?"

Tank nodded and ran a hand over his face. "Yeah. It's probably way too big for just me, but I like it. Good neighborhood."

They parted ways, and Ryder chuckled at what the neighbors must think of Tank moving in next door. Probably huddling their kids under their arms. It was their loss, though, because Tank was one of the kindest people he'd ever met. Once you saw past the Hulk exterior and rough edges.

Ryder made his way to his best friend's office. Flint greeted him with a wide smile and a bear hug.

"Good to see you, man," he said to Flint. "Everything work out okay in Mexico?"

"Esta bien," Flint replied, slipping into Spanish. "We could have used you down there, but I'm forever grateful you were with Fiona."

"Me too. About that…" He looked up at Flint sheepishly.

"Yeah. About that." Flint crossed his arms in front

of him and leaned back to sit on his desk. "Do I need to ask you about your intentions?"

Ryder felt the heat creep up his neck. How did he tell his best friend he planned to marry his sister?

"Yes, I would be curious about that too." Ryder turned to find the source of the beautiful voice. Fiona stood at the doorway of her brother's office, gorgeous as ever in jeans and a T-shirt. Over the past two-and-a-half months, he'd seen Fiona in blazers and cocktail dresses and baggy pajamas. The truth was, her beauty was far deeper than her clothes or skin. The last two weeks, as she had embraced her imperfection and allowed people to see her true self, she'd only grown more radiant.

"What are you doing here?" he asked.

"She's having lunch with her big brother," Flint said with a booming laugh as he hugged his sister.

Ryder looked between the Raven siblings. Flint was as close to him as his own brother. And now Fiona? Well, he couldn't imagine life without her.

"That sounds like a great idea. I'm surprised you didn't mention it yesterday morning," he said to Fiona.

She shrugged. "It was a last-minute invitation. Usually, I would have brushed it off, but I'm turning a new leaf, and I kind of like being spontaneous."

His mind couldn't help but slip back to the wedding reception three years ago, when he'd invited Fiona to steal the getaway car. "Come on, be spontaneous," he had challenged her.

The phone rang and Flint moved to answer it, leaving them near the door together.

Now, he returned the reply she'd given. "What happened to spontaneity is just irresponsibility in disguise?"

She tilted her head. "I was wrong. Back then, I thought being spontaneous meant admitting that I didn't have it all planned out. And that was unacceptable. I'm learning that sometimes it just means seizing an opportunity you didn't expect."

He wrapped his arms around her waist and kissed her firmly.

"And that's a good thing?"

"That can be a very good thing," she said. He kissed her again, and she sighed contentedly. "I never expected you, Ryder."

"I've always thought that was more fun. But I'm starting to come around to the idea that making plans is good too." He leaned in to whisper in her ear. "As a matter of fact, I've got a few ideas for plans of my own…"

"Can you get your hands off my sister? I'm standing right here, dude."

Ryder left his hands where they were, but he did step back slightly and grinned at his friend. "No promises, Rave. I'm crazy about her."

Flint stuck his finger in his mouth in a mocking gag gesture, but then laughed and came closer. He threw an arm around each of them and forced himself in between.

"I see how it is. Go on, take your sister to lunch. Then, I'll be here to take her to dinner." He turned to Fiona. "You are staying the night, right?"

She smiled. "Yeah, I am. Actually, I'm looking at some office space nearby tomorrow."

Ryder couldn't fight the grin that spread across his face. "You are?"

She nodded. "I think it's time Raven Foods left Manhattan behind. I hear Alexandria is nice."

CHAPTER TWENTY-EIGHT

RYDER OPENED the manila envelope at the counter, while Fiona cooked something that smelled fantastic in the spacious kitchen of his Alexandria condo. The return address was from New York City, and he had a sinking feeling he knew what it was.

The papers slid out onto the counter, and Ryder began to read the first page. A news article from nine years ago.

"New York City Girls Held Captive in Real Life Nightmare"

A post-it note attached to the page read only, "Trust your gut."

He poured over the pages, reading every word he could about the women from that house. The most recent was a news article from last year. One of the women had opened a victim's advocacy center in the city.

Fiona's hands slid around his shoulders and down his chest as she leaned in behind him.

"What's up? You're miles away."

He stared at the smiling face of the woman in the photo. "Bailey sent me the rest of the story."

"She sounds incredible," Fiona commented, with a finger on the printed article.

He nodded. But acid tore at the lining of his stomach. If only he would have done more and gotten them out sooner. The first articles—the ones published after the arrest and during Mr. Brighton's trial—had detailed their abuse in horrid detail. An entire additional year passed after his visit until they were found.

"What's wrong?" Fiona's sweet words made him close his eyes. How could such beauty and such evil coexist in this world? It didn't make him believe in God less, or even doubt God's goodness. But he would never really understand in his soul why this had to be the way it happened.

"I just… I should have found them when I was there. What they had to go through…" He heard the tortured sound in his own words.

Fiona must have heard it too, because she pulled

the papers from his hand and set them on the counter, before turning him around to face her. With a hand on either side of his face, she met his eyes. Ryder stared back at the beautiful brown Italian espresso of hers.

Then she tipped her forehead to his. "This was not your fault. There is nothing to forgive yourself for."

He shut his eyes. So many misdeeds of his past still haunted him. Choices he made…or didn't make.

She continued. "But even if there were… You once told me that we all make mistakes. We give grace to each other. But you also have to forgive yourself." She stroked his jaw, and he felt the love in her touch. "I know you think you have something to make up for, but you don't have to redeem yourself. Jesus already did that for you. For all of us."

He knew he would never deserve the blessings he'd been given. The friendship of people who never gave up on him and the protection in situations where he definitely should have died. And especially the gift of Fiona in his life.

Ryder pulled her onto his lap and wrapped his arms around her. "Thank you."

Fiona snuggled into the crook of his neck and made a contented sound as he ran a hand down her back.

"I love you, princess."

He felt her smile. "I love you, too."

Maybe he hadn't realized that all those blessings were only indicators, pointing him toward the greatest gift of all: reconciliation with God and true redemption from all his sins. Past, present, and future.

And when he looked to the future, he saw himself there alongside Fiona. Now that they finally found each other, he wasn't letting go. He'd be there for her every day, loving her. imperfect, beautiful soul. And he would protect her from anyone who might want to hurt her.

As a matter of fact, he had a few loose ends to tie up in that regard.

He pressed a kiss to her hairline. Tomorrow was soon enough.

EPILOGUE

RYDER WAITED SILENTLY, hidden in the dark shadows of the study in the fancy Georgetown home. He rubbed the smooth finish of his Beretta 92 to center himself. Tonight, Ryder had to be someone he hadn't been for many years. He'd called in a few more favors at the NYPD to get some time alone with Officer Chenoweth. That conversation, coupled with what Fiona had told him from Timperley's rantings, had led him here.

The expensive leather club chair he sat in belonged to Senator Katrina Morris. The esteemed senator would not appreciate Ryder's visit. But he'd spent the last two weeks spending every spare moment tracking the roots of Fiona's attack. The

Syndicate was undoubtedly bigger than Senator Morris, but she surely had a seat at the table.

His best guess for motive? Her husband's multi-billion dollar food conglomerate would surely benefit from one less competitor. In fact, Morris Foods had been in the news this morning for the acquisition of yet another small food manufacturer, this one in South Carolina. Using Syndicate ties—like hiring a secret subsidiary of Citadel—and tipping her hand to Cheno had allowed them to tie her back to the organization.

Quiet footsteps approached the study, and Ryder pointed the pistol at the door. The lights flipped on, and Senator Morris froze midstep.

"Don't move. Don't speak."

Ryder gestured to the chair across from him. "Sit. If you make a move, I will put a bullet between your eyes." He waited while Morris sat down. The woman remained rigid and tense, no doubt unused to having a gun pointed at her. "Do you know who I am, Senator?"

Morris shook her head.

"Good. But that means you don't know what I am capable of. I know you, though. I know about your hidden accounts in the Caymans and how you bribed your way onto the Foreign Affairs committee. I even know about your quiet affair with the young lawyer from Alexandria." He clicked his tongue in admonishment.

He slipped the safety off the gun.

"Listen carefully. Morris Foods, Citadel, and The Syndicate will abandon all efforts to harm Fiona Raven. Do you understand?"

Morris nodded.

"From what I can tell, Senator, you are a very smart woman. And you are probably thinking that you can outsmart us." Ryder filled his voice with the anger and determination he'd been consumed with after finding out The Syndicate was behind the entire scheme. "I'm telling you right now that would be a mistake. We will be watching your every move. And unless you call off the dogs, we *will* destroy you."

"W-what if they don't listen to me?"

Ryder clenched his jaw. She wanted to act like she wasn't in charge? He'd let her pretend. "Make them listen. I'll be in touch to make sure you do."

————

Cole Kensington signed the check and slipped his card back in his wallet.

"I've known you for a long time, Flint. You know

I appreciate everything you and Black Tower have done for me. But this one…it's tricky."

Flint nodded from his seat across the small table. The cozy lounge was tucked inside an old building, steps from the brick-lined sidewalks of King Street in Old Town Alexandria. "I understand. But you've got to protect your company."

Cole nodded, but it was more than that. Zia Pharmaceuticals was more than just a company. They changed peoples' lives. He might not be in the lab as a researcher anymore, but the work they did was still why he did it. And why he'd been resistant to the offers of acquisition.

But there was something going on, and he needed to get to the bottom of it. Which was where Black Tower Security came in.

"So, you've got a plan?"

Flint nodded. "I've got the perfect person. If you can get Joey plugged in as some systems analyst or security specialist…" He waved a hand. "Basically anything with computers and you'll be set."

Cole nodded. "That's easy enough. And you're sure Joey is the right one for the job? I *have* to find the mole."

"Joey is the one you want. If there is something

hidden in your systems or someone stealing information, Joey will find it…or them."

Cole sighed in relief. Knowing that someone Flint trusted would be on the job was already reassuring. "Good. I'll want personal updates about what he finds."

Flint smirked.

He tipped his head. "What? Something I said?"

"No. It's just that… You should know – Joey's a woman."

Cole mentally rearranged the assumptions he'd already made.

Flint leaned forward. "Joey is the best hacker I've ever seen. She worked for me at Raven Tech…and well, let's just say before that she was wearing a different color hat."

Cole raised his eyebrows. "But you trust her?"

Flint nodded. "With my life."

"Well, all right then. When can I meet her?" He needed to size this woman up for himself. Especially if he was going to let her inside the fortified walls of Zia's network.

Flint glanced across the room and signaled someone with a head nod. She was here?

When he realized the woman walking toward

them was actually walking *toward them,* his mouth went dry.

Initially, he'd been expecting to create a cover for a pale-skinned, balding guy with a soft belly who would fade into the woodwork of the IT department. When Flint had said Joey was a woman, he realized he'd simply switched the gender. It hadn't prepared him for the gorgeous woman in front of him. She would never fade into the woodwork. Anywhere.

Flint stood as she approached and Cole scrambled to do the same. "Cole Kensington, may I introduce Josephina Rodriguez?"

He caught the eyeroll she flashed her boss before she turned to meet him. "It's Joey." Her dark-brown eyes met his with a spark of laughter. This was the woman who could program circles around the team at Raven Tech?

He held out his hand. "Nice to meet you, Joey."

————

Joey considered a moment before taking his offered hand. She'd seen his photo a dozen times as she looked through news articles, but he was taller in person. And more handsome. He'd worked his way up in the company from researcher to Technical Director and taken over the reins from the previous owner and CEO. Now, he owned a 30% stake in the company that was on the forefront of cancer and Alzheimer's research. Rich, smart, and good-looking?

Why was the world so unfair?

At least she had the skills to help correct the imbalance. Flint hadn't mentioned why he wanted her at the meeting, but the CEO of the pharmaceutical giant was high on her list for suspected ties to The Syndicate. She knew they were just starting to unwind the web of The Syndicate and all the players. Digging through potential baddies, it seemed like every big-name corporate head was interconnected, along with every politician.

The list of potential members of The Syndicate was basically a list of Who's Who in America. And Cole Kensington was always sure to be included on that list. But he was a good friend of Flint's. If it turned out he was also Syndicate? Well, there would be an entire team of muscled ex-SWAT and military guys to take care of him. No doubt Ryder would be first in line.

At least for now, their team would be safe from The Syndicate. She'd make sure of it from her favorite spot–right behind her computer, where she kept an eye and an ear on everything. Just how she liked it.

"Nice to meet you, Mr. Kensington." She turned back to Flint. "You going to tell me what's going on? Let me guess." She looked the surprisingly muscular CEO from head to toe. "Mr. Kensington needs the paper trail of a secret baby to disappear?" His expression darkened and he began to shake his head. "Erase his presence from a flight? Adjust his previous tax returns? Get the city to lose his parking tickets?"

Cole's expression turned to one of laughter, then he paused. "You can do that?"

She shrugged. "Which one? The IRS? Easy. Delta Airlines? Slightly harder, but yeah. I can do that. So, what is it, Raven?" She'd like to get this over with and get back to her desk. That was where she could protect her team. Being out here was a waste of her time. She trusted Flint without question, though. So here she was. "This seems like it could have been an e-mail," she referenced Raven's favorite mug with the saying. He hated unnecessary time wasted in meetings.

Flint gestured for them all to sit down. "I wanted to do this in person. You've got a new assignment,

Joey. Starting Monday, you'll be a full-time employee at Zia Pharmaceuticals."

Continue Reading Joey and Cole's story in Hostile Intent.

NOTE TO READERS

Thank you for picking up (or downloading!) this book. If you enjoyed it, please consider taking a minute to leave a review or rating. I hope you are looking forward to Joey and Cole's story as much as I am. I think they have a lot to teach each other.

Speaking of being taught -- my first foray into romantic suspense taught me so much! I had so much fun telling the story, allowing the twists and turns to surprise me along the way also. It stretched me, and I look forward to growing in my suspense story craft as I move forward with this series.

Fiona and Ryder's struggles with perfectionism and grace are rooted in my own. While I attempted to write this story with a lighter faith arc, I made it to the end of the story and realized that Ryder couldn't truly forgive himself without fully steeping in the grace of Jesus. Once again, the Lord proved that no matter the question – the answer is Him.

Ryder also struggled with understanding why such trauma and evil exists. And as I write this note, the world is face to face with the ugly reality of war in Ukraine as well as ongoing violence and humanitarian crises in Syria, Sudan, Afghanistan, and more. I've been wrestling with the Lord about the wickedness in the world, even more than the struggle with a broken world in disease and natural disasters.

Reading the news, local or global, gives far too many examples of pure, unbridled evil around us. It's abhorrent and terrifying and heartbreaking to see innocent people suffer the consequences of an evil person.

But God is still good.

Even in war. Even in the terminal diagnosis. Even in the abuse.

His heart breaks.

He loves you.

God is a much more capable author than me. And just like in my books -- evil doesn't win in the end. Justice and victory and eternal glory are His, Amen.

I pray my books encourage you in your faith and through your struggles, whatever they may be. I love hearing the amazing ways God has used my words in the lives of my readers. It is incredibly humbling and encouraging! You can email me anytime at taragraceericson@gmail.com.

You can learn more about my upcoming projects at my website: www.taragraceericson.com or by signing up for my newsletter. Just for signing up, you'll get two free stories, including Clean Slate, the introduction to the Black Tower Security Series. It's the story of what happened with Flint and Jessica before BTS was formed. Sign up to start reading it today.

If you've never read my other books, I'd love for you to read the Main Street Minden Series and dive into the world of Minden, Indiana.

Thank you again for all your support and encouragement.

ACKNOWLEDGMENTS

Above all – Thank you, God. Without your blessings and direction, these books would never exist. You are so incredibly faithful.

To my content editor, Jessica from BH Writing Services. Having you dissect my stories has taught me so much, and made each one incalculably better.

To my copy editor, Brandi. You do an incredible job and I'm so thankful for you!

To Hannah Jo Abbott and Mandi Blake, for being the best accountability, prayer, and venting partners a girl could ask for.

And to the rest of our Author Circle -- Jess Mastorakos, Elizabeth Maddrey and K Leah. Iron sharpens iron. I'm so grateful for each of you.

Special thanks to Jess Mastorakos for making the gorgeous covers for this series and swapping a thousand iterations of them with me online. You're so talented.

To Deana for her amazing photography skills and for hooking me up with the sweetest cover models.

And to Shay and Troy for letting me use their picture on the cover. Congratulations on your happily ever after!

To Gabbi. Because you've been asking for more suspense with every book.

To my parents, for being a wonderful example of love, faith, and hard work. Especially to my mother, for being my extra set of eyes (and ears) for every story!

Thank you to all my readers, without whose support and encouragement, I would have given up a long time ago.

To all the other bloggers, bookstagrammers, and reviewers who read my books and share your thoughts. Thank you from the bottom of my heart.

And finally, to my husband. Our life is loud and busy, and I relish our quiet moments together. I repeatedly wonder why God blessed me with a partner I so completely don't deserve. Thank you for your grace, your encouragement, and your back scratches.

Mr. B – Stay kind, sweet boy. You are growing up so fast. But you are never too old for a hug from your mom.

Little C – You are unstoppable. You are so funny

and smart. Blaze your own path, little one, I'll be there for you. Always.

And Baby L – Your sweet smile melts my heart. You are so loved.

BLACK TOWER SECURITY

CLEAN SLATE

Read Clean Slate for free today by signing up for Tara's newsletter and find out how Black Tower Security came to be.

She's running for her life. He can't lose her again.

Personal trainer Jessica Street has stumbled into a money laundering scheme at her gym, and the people responsible aren't too happy about the extra liability. To make matters worse, the only person who can help her is the one man she never wants to see again.

Flint Raven regrets breaking Jessica's heart ten years ago when he chose his career over her. But the former security tech mogul isn't the man he used to be. When bullets start flying, he knows he'll do anything to protect her and prove he's worthy of a second chance.

Jessica has no choice to accept his help. But she's determined to protect her heart while Flint is protecting her life.

HOSTILE INTENT

Black Tower Security Book 2 – Hostile Intent, available for Pre-order now!

He hired her to find out who is spilling corporate secrets.
She's determined to find out his.

When Black Tower Security sends Joey Rodriguez undercover at Zia Pharmaceuticals, she has her own motives for agreeing to the assignment – namely, to prove to her boss that Cole Kensington isn't what he seems.

Cole has always had one goal—a cure for Alzheimer's. Now that he and his company are close, he's got a big problem. Corporate espionage in the pharmaceutical industry is par for the course, but this time he called for help. The undercover hacker they sent gets under his skin, but she is supposed to be the best—and he needs the best. Cole won't let a spy in his ranks jeopardize something this important.

Helping a billionaire wasn't what Joey signed up for. But as she starts to untangle the web of secrets and spies inside Zia, she finds herself in the crosshairs—and trusting the very man she hoped to expose.

ABOUT THE AUTHOR

Tara Grace Ericson lives in Missouri with her husband and three sons. She studied engineering and worked as an engineer for many years before embracing her creative side to become a full-time author. Now, she spends her days chasing her boys and writing books when she can.

She loves cooking, crocheting, and reading books by the dozen. She loves a good "happily ever after" with an engaging love story. That's why Tara focuses on writing clean contemporary romance, with an emphasis on Christian faith and living. She wants to encourage her readers with stories of men and women who live out their faith in tough situations.

BOOKS BY TARA GRACE ERICSON

Free Stories

Love and Chocolate

Clean Slate (Romantic Suspense)

The Main Street Minden Series

Falling on Main Street

Winter Wishes

Spring Fever

Summer to Remember

Kissing in the Kitchen: A Main Street Minden Novella

The Bloom Sisters Series

Hoping for Hawthorne - A Bloom Family Novella

A Date for Daisy

Poppy's Proposal

Lavender and Lace

Longing for Lily

Resisting Rose

Dancing with Dandelion